What Stalks
the Deep

TOR BOOKS BY T. KINGFISHER

Nettle & Bone
Thornhedge
A Sorceress Comes to Call
Swordheart
A House With Good Bones
Hemlock & Silver

THE SWORN SOLDIER SERIES
What Moves the Dead
What Feasts at Night

T. KINGFISHER

What Stalks the Deep

Tor Publishing Group
New York

This is a work of fiction. All of the characters, organizations, and events portrayed in this novella are either products of the author's imagination or are used fictitiously.

WHAT STALKS THE DEEP

Copyright © 2025 by Ursula Vernon

All rights reserved.

Endpaper art by Ursula Vernon

A Nightfire Book
Published by Tom Doherty Associates / Tor Publishing Group
120 Broadway
New York, NY 10271

www.torpublishinggroup.com

Nightfire™ is a trademark of Macmillan Publishing Group, LLC.

EU Representative: Macmillan Publishers Ireland Ltd, 1st Floor, The Liffey Trust Centre, 117–126 Sheriff Street Upper, Dublin 1, DO1 YC43

The Library of Congress Cataloging-in-Publication Data is available upon request.

ISBN 978-1-250-35492-1 (hardcover)
ISBN 978-1-250-35493-8 (ebook)

The publisher of this book does not authorize the use or reproduction of any part of this book in any manner for the purpose of training artificial intelligence technologies or systems. The publisher of this book expressly reserves this book from the Text and Data Mining exception in accordance with Article 4(3) of the European Union Digital Single Market Directive 2019/790.

Our books may be purchased in bulk for specialty retail/wholesale, literacy, corporate/premium, educational, and subscription box use. Please contact MacmillanSpecialMarkets@macmillan.com.

First Edition: 2025

Printed in the United States of America

10 9 8 7 6 5 4 3 2

To Cousin Amy

What Stalks the Deep

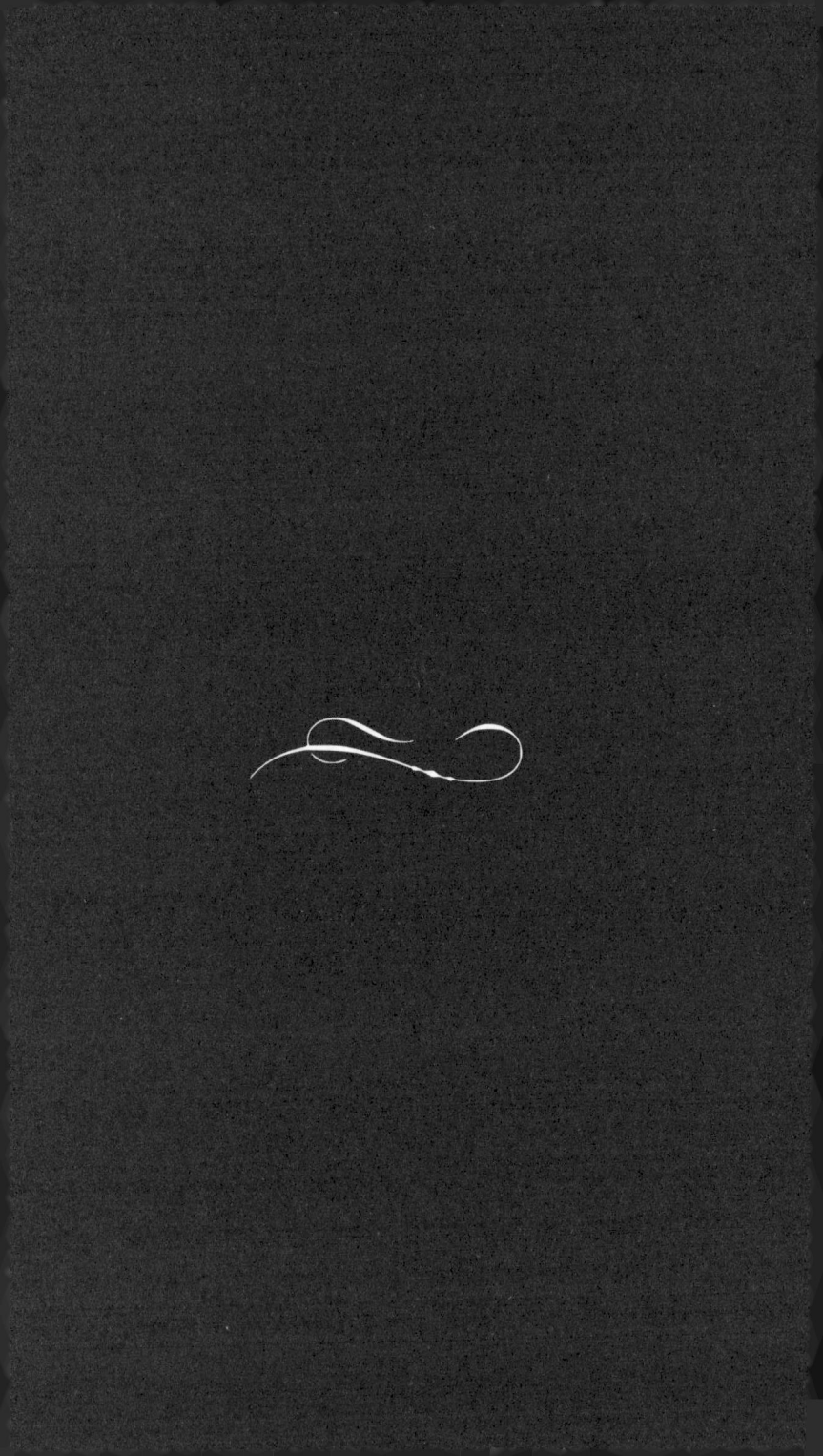

CHAPTER 1

So this was America. Fresh off the war with Spain, which was all that anybody was talking about. Guam. Everyone on the ship over had been full of opinions about Guam. Several people asked my opinion "as a military man." They were wrong about the man part, but the thought of explaining Gallacia's sworn soldiers to a boatload of Americans was so exhausting that I needed a gin and tonic just to contemplate it, and a second one to decide that explaining would be a bad idea.

As for Guam, my opinion was that it was probably a fine place and the weather was undoubtedly better than in Gallacia. I developed the habit of smiling down into my gin and tonic and saying that I had never been to Guam, and so wouldn't presume to know more than the people on the ground there. This had the advantage of being true, and also generally made at least one other person in the conversation look like an absolute tit.

And if I passed our days at sea having gin and tonics and no opinions about Guam, that meant I was definitely not worrying about the telegram that I had been sent by my American friend, Dr. James Denton.

BEGGING YOU TO COME WITH ALL HASTE STOP NEED YOUR HELP STOP BRING ANGUS STOP

If it had been anyone other than Denton, I would have sent back another telegram to the effect of "What the devil is the problem stop?" but Denton and I had faced down horrors together two years prior, and I knew that he had a cool head and was, if anything, far more skeptical than I was. If he thought he needed my help, then I would damn well come and help him. Also, he included two tickets to Boston.

(Also, my sister was going to have *another* child and while I think babies are fine in the abstract, my sister has a regrettable belief that if I just hold one long enough, I will come to enjoy it. I will not. I have proven this to my own satisfaction, but apparently not to hers, and America seemed like an excellent alternative. Land of opportunity, they say, which presumably includes the opportunity *not* to hold a baby.)

I say this all very flippantly, but I'll be honest, I didn't much care for the telegram. Not that I objected to Denton asking for my help—far from it. There are some experiences that bond people together more closely than blood, and the nightmare we'd faced had been one of them. If he needed my help, I'd come.

No, what bothered me was the idea that whatever trouble Denton was in, it was the sort of trouble that required Angus and me to cross an ocean. As if, given the entire North American continent to draw from, Denton needed the two people he knew with experience in nightmares.

I tried not to dwell on it, and instead lost myself in listening to people be wrong about Guam. It almost worked.

Our ship steamed into Boston on a brisk October morning. The sun was shining, the water was relatively calm for the season, and the air smelled only slightly of brine and dead fish. Our crossing had been uneventful, our docking equally so. The jaws of the wharf closed over our ship and held it fast. The streets of Boston looked like the streets of any other port town I've encountered. It could have been London or Hamburg. Make half the people darker and half the walls lighter, and you could be in Barcelona or Istanbul. Skin and stone changes, but not much else does. There are always children pelting around and harried-looking men moving cargo into wagons and a few extremely worried men who do not have cargo and don't know why and a dozen horses looking bored and one horse looking like it is about to go on a rampage and a couple of lost passengers huddled together like a clutch of baby chicks. Inevitably, a vendor is trying to sell something to one or more of these groups, except possibly the horses.

The familiarity was oddly comforting. In general I rather like Americans—they're usually so terribly earnest—but I'd be lying if I said I wasn't a bit nervous. One American can really fill a room. I assume it only takes a hundred or so to really fill a country.

A man threaded his way through this mess, avoiding the

vendor, and approached us. He was fine-boned and neatly dressed, like a small bird wearing a clean, unassuming suit.

"You must be Lieutenant Easton," he said, shaking first my hand and then Angus's. "I'm Kent, Dr. Denton's assistant. I'm to see you to the hotel where you'll be meeting him and Mr. Ingold."

"Lead on, then," I said, trading a look with Angus. We don't shake hands in Gallacia, but Americans are completely mad for it, and you can't refuse or they get this confused, somewhat hurt look. I resigned myself to shaking a great many hands in the next few weeks.

Kent secured a cab. Angus and I hefted our luggage onto the roof. "Is that all?" asked Kent. "No more trunks? No equipment?"

"We travel light," I said, wondering what sort of equipment he expected me to bring. Angus had the rifle case. Did that count as equipment? Or did he think that all Europeans were like the upper-class Brits, and had five different outfits for each meal of the day?

(Come to think of it, maybe Americans did that, too. If so, thank God I'd brought one of my dress uniforms. You can always get away with wearing a dress uniform instead of formalwear. Although Denton had never struck me as a formalwear type. Someone who would help you finish off a fungal abomination that had taken over your childhood friend, yes. Someone who wore a tuxedo with tails to dinner, not so much.)

Our cab left the docks, trotting past rows of horse-drawn streetcars. We don't have those in Gallacia. Then again, we don't have that much flat ground in Gallacia. It is a very small country made of very large mountains. We grow turnips and sheep, but our primary export is people who want to get the hell away from it.

I was farther away now than I'd ever been. "I don't suppose you'd care to tell me what this is all about?" I asked Kent.

Kent folded his hands neatly on his knee. "I am certain that Dr. Denton will explain everything when you arrive."

So much for that. Angus might have been able to get more out of him, if they'd been alone and doing the "Oh yeah? Well, *my* boss once made me carry kan ten miles in the snow because ka was too cheap to hire a horse!" dance, but it didn't look like we'd have time.

We eventually reached a medium-sized hotel. Kent paid the driver and helped Angus pull down the luggage, and we followed him inside.

"That is a *lot* of mauve," I said, after a moment of stunned silence. The wallpaper was mauve, the carpet that stretched across the marble floor was mauve, the draperies were mauve, the upholstery was mauve, and the pillows scattered on the furniture were mauve with gold tassels. I suddenly knew how a bee must feel with its head buried in a mallow flower.

Kent waved to the front desk and a man came out from behind it, wearing a mauve tie. He shook our hands and said that it was the hotel's great pleasure to serve us. He clapped his hands and summoned a bellhop, dressed from head to toe in mauve, who took our luggage. I wondered if the bellhops ever stood up against the walls for camouflage.

The hotel man shook our hands again and pressed our keys into them at the same time, in a skilled maneuver that I assume required years of experience. "Dr. Denton is waiting for you in the dining room," said Kent, herding us efficiently to one side of the lobby. We entered the dining room, which had mauve tablecloths, and I spotted my old friend Denton, who, thank Christ, was wearing a dark brown suit and no mauve at all.

He rose to his feet and shook our hands. "Easton. Angus. I'm so glad you agreed to come."

"From the tone of your telegram, I expected you to be hip-deep in live wasps," I said, "not dining at such a . . . ah . . . *colorful* establishment."

"We'll get to the wasps in a moment," said Denton. "May I introduce my friend, Mr. John Ingold? John, this is Lieutenant Alex Easton and Angus . . . ah . . . forgive me, it occurs to me that I don't actually know your full name."

"No one does," said Angus gruffly.

I hid a smile. Angus has been with me since I was a scrawny fourteen-year-old with a shaved head and bound breasts who barely knew which end to hold a gun by. In all that time, I had never learned if Angus was his first or last name or where he came from originally. If he ever wants me to know, I imagine he'll tell me.

"Pleasure to meet you both," said John Ingold, reaching across the table to shake our hands. He had the tan skin and straight black hair that I associate with the native people of the continent, and when he opened his mouth, his Boston accent was so thick that you could stand a spoon up in it. (Yes, we know about Boston accents in Gallacia. We're backward, but we do occasionally meet people.)

(Okay, fine, I met a Bostonian in Paris once.)

The waiter approached. I half expected him to go in for a handshake as well, but he merely asked for our orders, then retreated into the mauve distance.

"So," I said, putting my elbows on the table and looking at Denton. "What has you so concerned?"

Denton rubbed his face. "It's a mess," he said.

"Dark doings," Ingold added. The way he pronounced *dark* as *dahhhk* was so pure that I had an involuntary urge to snatch up the teapot and find a harbor to dump it in.

"My cousin Oscar's gone missing," said Denton. "We grew up together, and we were in very regular correspondence until his letters stopped three weeks ago. I sent an additional two letters, and then went to West Virginia myself to try to find him."

I settled back against the exceedingly mauve cushions. "I'm sorry to hear it, but you must know, Denton, that I'm no kind of detective."

"No, of course not." Denton shook his head. "I know exactly where he vanished. He was investigating an abandoned coal mine outside of Shaversville. That's what I need you to help me with."

"I've never been in a coal mine in my life," I protested.

"I have," said Angus. "In Limburg. Was dark as the pit and we had to walk bent over."

We all waited politely for him to say anything more, but this seemed to have exhausted Angus's store of coal mine information. Denton coughed. "At any rate, it's your experience with . . . unusual . . . circumstances that I need."

I raised an eyebrow. Angus raised both of his. "You mean like what we saw at Usher's lake," I said flatly. "Because I'll tell you, that was the first time I've dealt with anything like that." (Sadly it was not the last, but what had happened a year ago in Gallacia was not something I wanted to dwell on.)

"The first time for me, too," said Denton. He looked suddenly weary and much older than I remembered. "But you *did* deal with it, and you know there are terrible things in the earth. If you encounter another one, you won't waste time insisting that there must be a different explanation or that I'm lying to you or that none of this can possibly be happening."

Terrible things in the earth. Yes. Denton and I had seen a terrible thing in the earth and ended it, with the help of Angus and a brilliant Englishwoman who knew everything worth knowing about mushrooms. The only reason that I slept at night was because we *had* destroyed it. I did not want there to be another one.

"Another fungus?" I asked sharply.

Denton drank down his whiskey and signaled for another one. Ingold watched me, his arms folded, and I wondered how much Denton had told him about what we saw in the tarn.

"Not a fungus," Denton said, when the waiter had left again. "At least, I don't think so. But more lights in the deep."

CHAPTER 2

"About two months ago, my cousin Oscar went to Hollow Elk Mine in West Virginia," Denton said, "looking to see if there was any coal left."

I sipped my gin and tonic and waited. His mention of lights in the deep had taken me back, forcibly, to Usher's lake, to the brilliant, terrible stars that glowed in the depths of the tarn. It was not a memory I cherished.

"Everything here runs on coal," Ingold explained. "During the War Between the States, the South ran their warships on coal from the Carolinas. The North ramped up production in West Virginia to compensate, and never stopped. Now you'll hardly find a hillside that somebody's not sinking a mine into."

"But this one was abandoned?" I asked.

Ingold nodded. "Hollow Elk Mine is a bit east of Shaversville, dug in the 1700s. Old place, but the ground was bad. Rockfalls, cave-ins, the lot. Miners said it was unlucky."

"Some of them said it was haunted," put in Denton.

"Any unlucky mine is haunted," said Ingold dismissively. "You kill enough men with bad food and bad air, the earth soaks that up. What my mother's people would call bad medicine. I doubt Hollow Elk is worse than any other in that regard. No, there was more at work here. Miners reported strange lights in the deep, not just the usual knocking and tapping one gets in a working mine. It was abandoned about forty years later. The owners couldn't get enough people to work it, and by the end they were losing money on it. It reopened briefly during the war, but closed right up again."

"Who are the owners now?" asked Angus.

"You're looking at him," said Denton. He leaned back with a sigh. "Oscar, God love him, always liked digging, whether it was papers or actual dirt. He was going through our family's old papers when he found the deed to the mine. I hadn't even known I'd inherited it. No one's given it any thought for at least a generation, I imagine. Hollow Elk had been abandoned, and hadn't been worth much even when fully up and running, according to the papers. Oscar was curious as to why it had been abandoned." Denton took a gulp of whiskey. If I didn't know better, I'd think his eyes were getting misty, which was surprising, because Denton was not a misty-eyed type.

"When Oscar and I were kids, he was always looking for caves. Got stuck in one when he was twelve and it took the fire department three hours to get him out again. Then he was back in there the next week. So when he asked if I'd mind if he took a look at the old mine, I didn't think twice. He said he wanted to see if there was any money to be made from it, with more modern mining techniques, but I knew mostly he just wanted an excuse to go poking around underground. Caves, mines, that sort of thing—he was mad for them." Denton looked up at me, a wry, unhappy twist to his lips. "So you see, this is ultimately my fault."

I raised a skeptical eyebrow at that. "Did he have experience underground?" Angus asked. "Other than getting stuck?"

"Quite a lot, yes."

Angus and I exchanged a look. "Then I don't see how you could be blamed, unless there's a lot more to the story," I said.

The line between Denton's eyes didn't smooth out. "He sent me a number of letters," he said. "The first few aren't particularly noteworthy. He reached the mine, set up camp there, and began mapping out the details. Then, almost a month after he arrived, he sent me this." Denton nodded to Kent, who extracted a sheaf of notes from his valise and handed them to me.

I unfolded the letter. It was written in a neat, even hand, the sort of lettering beloved of clerks and teachers.

James—
I must apologize for what I am about to commit to paper, for it must seem as if I am springing it upon you without warning. In truth, I have been observing these phenomena since the very beginning of my exploration of Hollow Elk, but I have been reluctant to mention them. They were easily dismissed at first

as the tricks a man's mind plays on him in the dark, and I did dismiss them as such, until the evidence began to weigh too heavily against it.

Ah, I thought. The sort of person who talks about "observing phenomena." I actually quite like people like that, because if you can get them talking about their particular specialty, they will tell you the most fascinating anecdotes about botflies or ball lightning or things they have extracted from some unfortunate soul's rectum. They can be immense fun at otherwise stuffy parties.

I have been hearing sounds in the mine. Not the creaks or knocks that are common to mines, but peculiar sounds, as of something moving around within it. The mine entrance is large and the boards did not cover it completely, so I was not surprised by this either, suspecting only that some animal had taken up residence within. But of late the sounds have gotten closer, and there is something damnably odd about them. They are wet sounds, almost a squelching. Roger hears them too, so I have at least that much proof that it is not my imagination.

Furthermore, things have been going missing. Sheets of paper and at least two fountain pens have vanished, as well as several tins of stew. Roger denies taking any of it, and certainly he is not a man to steal paper and pen. Indeed, I should be overjoyed to find a newfound tendency to literacy in him, and would happily gift him entire reams! (I do suspect him in the case of the stew. He has lately acquired an enormous mutt from the nearby town, and I have no doubt that it eats like a horse. I do not begrudge the dog the stew, though, as it is a comfort to have a watchdog about.)

Ordinarily I would not trouble you with such minor matters, as the noises have continued off and on for weeks, and may be nothing more disconcerting than a drip behind a wall, or a frog having taken up residence in some flooded subsection, and of course, things go missing everywhere, most particularly pens. But yesterday, while I was mapping the lowest area in the third level—the last area excavated before the mine was abandoned—I saw something impossible in the depths. I saw light.

I cannot explain to you how unsettling it was. When you are deep underground, light can only mean other people. There was no possibility of a shaft from above intersecting with this one. This level was not ventilated before being abandoned. Furthermore, the light was red. Deep red, like a darkroom light. I had turned off my own carbide headlamp to refill it, and at first I thought my eyes were playing tricks on me, but there was indeed a red light much farther down the tunnel. It did not flicker like firelight, but was strong and steady.

I am not one of those men who carries a pistol wherever he goes, certainly not within a cave system. But I tell you, James, I wished that I had one then. There was something desperately frightening about seeing a light underground where no light should be. I thought of a dozen improbable explanations, mostly involving lava—you'll laugh at that, and I would too—but I could think of nothing that could realistically explain such a light.

Very likely I should have gone to fetch Roger to explore the tunnel with me. But at the time, all I could think was that if I did not go at once, whoever made the light could follow me up the sloping shaft to the higher levels, lie in wait there, and then come down behind me the next time I ventured in. I could not bear the thought, and so I redonned my carbide lamp and went forward toward the light.

I will spare you suspense. I did not find the source. It went out almost as soon as my own light went on. The main tunnel here splits into three passages, and I picked the wrong one initially, only to reach a dead end. The central tunnel ends in a squeeze and I would have had to crawl through on hands and knees in order to continue. I am nearly certain, however, that the red light was on the far side of the squeeze. When I turned my own light off again and waited, I heard something moving down there. It dislodged dirt and pebbles, whatever it was, and I do not think that it was the sound of further subsidence.

I would think that it was an animal, but animals do not wear lights.

At any rate, James, you doubtless think that I have gone off my head from bad air now, and I cannot say that I blame you. Certainly Roger is skeptical, although he is too loyal to say anything of the sort, and the dog he's acquired has given no indication of any strangers about. The brute even barks at passing deer and rabbits, so I doubt any human could pass unmarked.

Nevertheless, I plan to get to the bottom of this. The squeeze is a small one, as blasting on this level was not far advanced, and while the air is hardly pleasant, it is not so bad as to make one hallucinate. No, I think some person has taken up residence in the mine itself. I plan to investigate further, if it is possible to do so without the ceiling falling in on me. Rest assured that I will take all due precautions, and shall update you as I can.

Yr devoted cousin,
Oscar

I handed the last page to Angus, feeling an odd clenching in my gut. Not so much at the contents—I could think of a half dozen explanations off the top of my head, including very ordinary human thieves—but the word *squeeze* came and squatted inside my chest in a way that I didn't like.

"What is this *squeeze* he's referring to?" I asked.

"Ah," said Ingold. "In a mine like Hollow Elk, they leave pillars of rock between excavations to hold up the ceiling. If the weight of the ceiling is too great, it bears down on the pillars and the floor rises toward the ceiling, so the passage becomes very narrow."

"That is horrifying and I want to go home," I said, although I pronounced it, "Ah. I see."

Despite the formal tone of the letter, it was far too easy to put myself in Oscar's shoes. I could imagine the weight of all that rock overhead, pressing down, *squeezing* . . .

I have never thought of myself as claustrophobic. It hadn't occurred to me that maybe I just had never been required to test that.

The waiter appeared at my elbow with another gin and

tonic before I noticed that my glass was empty. Funny how that works sometimes. Denton thanked him absently, his eyes distant. I suspected that in his head, he was a great many miles away, underground, watching strange lights.

The next letter was dated two days later, and the handwriting was notably less even, with occasional blobs of ink.

Denton—

I have found the strangest thing in the mine—or more accurately, behind the mine. It is all so peculiar that I am dashing off this note at once, lest I start to doubt my own recollections. Undoubtedly you will doubt them as well! If you come here, though, and I wish that you would, I will show you what I am referring to.

I am sorry, I am telling it all out of order. I went through the squeeze and found, as I had half expected, that mining had stopped on the far side. The coal seam had run out and these tunnels were mostly exploratory to see if they could pick it up again elsewhere. But it was not a dead end, as I had believed. There was a gap in the stone, amid the rubble left over, though it seemed so narrow that only a boy could fit through. I would have missed it entirely, but there was air coming through from the gap.

My first thought was that there was another mine nearby and that the shaft had broken into this one. But there are no nearby mines, so far as I know, and unless their shaft ran for miles underground, I would certainly be aware of it.

The other possibility—that this was somehow a nat-

ural cave—defied geology. Coal seams and caves do not coexist easily, particularly in this part of the world. Nevertheless, I will spare you suspense and tell you that it was a cave. How natural it is, I am not certain.

Roger had grave concerns about excavating the rubble, afraid that the ceiling would come down upon our heads. Given the squeeze, I cannot blame him. We put up timbers, which I confess most likely provided only psychological support, and began clearing the rubble.

The tunnel we found is low and broad, requiring one to traverse on hands and knees, sloping downward. The walls are very smooth, but of a curious, almost undulating shape, tapering inward for perhaps two feet before belling out again for another two, then back again. Despite the discomfort of crawling, it was a very easy passage, though it went for a remarkably long distance, moving downward in a gentle spiral. I could not determine if we were directly beneath the Hollow Elk Mine or if the spiral veered to one side or the other.

When it finally ended, it was at a tangle of limestone seamed with cracks. (By this I knew that we had gone down extremely far indeed.) It looked like a natural cave system, though many of the stalactites had fallen and broken, probably in recent times judging by the wear. But far more important was a passage leading upward to the right, from which light was emerging. Not the red light that I had seen before, but a steady white glow.

Denton, it was a marvel. A chamber a hundred

feet across, floored with some gemstone that I have never seen before. It was perfectly smooth, almost like glass, and shone like mother-of-pearl, and it glowed in the darkness, with a light strong enough to read by.

I have never seen anything like it. It was beautiful and impossible and it filled me with the awe and dread that only the inexplicable can invoke. I do not know how such a thing came to be.

The gemstone was too hard to break off, and Roger certainly tried his best. He did not like the cave though, pronouncing it "not canny."

You must come and see it, for I can hardly believe my own eyes and would be grateful for someone else's. Roger has many fine qualities, but objectivity is not among them.

That is the bulk of my discovery, and the most important thing. I will note in passing that on our return, I found the tins that had gone missing. They were in the small cave, each of them punctured in the middle and drained. So our mysterious thief is staying down here, although we did not see him during our visit.

Please come at once. This is an extraordinary find, and one which deserves to be brought before the eyes of men of learning.

*Yrs,
Oscar*

"Huh," I said, when I had reached the end and handed the last page to Angus. "A gemstone cavern underground? It sounds almost too fabulous to be true."

"You're not the only one to think so," Ingold muttered.

"Obviously I went down at once," Denton said. "He was nowhere to be found. I spent a day or two trying to find him, but no one had any leads at all. When I came back, this was waiting for me." He shoved a much-folded slip of paper across the table at me. I unfolded it and saw another telegram.

> MY APOLOGIES FOR HAVING MISSED YOU STOP I TOOK ILL FROM THE MINE GAS STOP PLEASE IGNORE MY PRIOR LETTERS AS I WAS NOT IN MY RIGHT MIND WHEN WRITING STOP HOLLOW ELK MINE IS OF NO INTEREST STOP

"Wordy fellow, your cousin," I said, passing the telegram to Angus. I would have used half as many words and paid a great deal less. Then again, perhaps this Oscar fellow was too wealthy to care.

"Wordy, yes," said Denton, "in letters, as you saw. But he writes telegrams the same as the rest of us . . . or he did."

"You don't think he wrote this one?" I hazarded.

"I'm nearly sure of it. For one thing, he hasn't responded to any of the letters I've sent after, and he hasn't sent any more of his own."

"Maybe he's embarrassed," rumbled Angus. "You go off your head on mine gas, you see things that aren't there and send wild letters about it? A man has a right to feel like a damn fool."

"Maybe," said Denton. "I'd have said that Oscar is more the type to make a joke out of it. But even so, he would never have said that the mine was of no interest. And even if that was true, he would simply have gone home. But his mother says that he hasn't been back, and he hasn't written to *her*, either. Trust me, Oscar could be off his head from mine gas, half dead, and missing both hands and he would *still* have written home to his mother."

I half smiled at that, but it turned into a frown. "I suppose that leaves the possibility that someone murdered him and sent the telegram to cover it up."

"That's what I think has happened," offered Ingold. "I grant that the letters about what he was finding are unsettling, but there's no reason to think it was anything but straightforward murder. He had an assistant. If there was something valuable in the mine and his assistant wanted it, he may have killed Oscar to get it."

There was a tightness around Denton's eyes, but he didn't protest the suggestion that his cousin was dead. I wondered if he had accepted the possibility, or if he and Ingold had simply argued it so many times that it no longer had the power to sting.

"Roger was incredibly loyal to Oscar," Denton said. "And yes, I know, men have turned their coats before. But Roger was also very nearly illiterate. He *couldn't* have sent that telegram."

"He got someone else to write it, then," argued Ingold. By the well-worn feel of the debate, I was pretty sure this wasn't the first time. "And that's why you've had no more letters. He knew he couldn't fake those."

Denton sighed. "Would you think less of me if I said that was what I hope happened? But the letters . . . and the mine." He rubbed his hands over his face. "There is something very wrong with that mine. I made the trek to West Virginia myself and found his gear and papers still there, but not Oscar. I only went a little way into the mine, just far enough to call for him, but it felt . . . wrong." He met my eyes across the table. "It felt like standing in Usher's house again. And you of all people, Easton, know that I don't say that lightly."

Usher's house. The creeping malignancy that had seemed to infest the walls there, made of more than just the library full of rotting books and the worms gnawing on the beams. The thing that had dwelt in the dark lake and sent fungal fingers up into the house itself. Yes, I knew.

The thought of facing such a thing again made me want to turn around and head straight to the docks for a ship going back to Europe. In fact, if there wasn't a ship, I might see how far I could swim.

But Denton had asked for my help, and there was nothing in me that would allow me to turn tail when a friend needed me. Ours is not to question why, etc. (I hate that poem, but I understand it.) Denton had stood beside me against the horrors in Usher's lake. It was my turn to stand beside him now.

I drained my gin and tonic and set it down. "All right," I said. "When do we leave?"

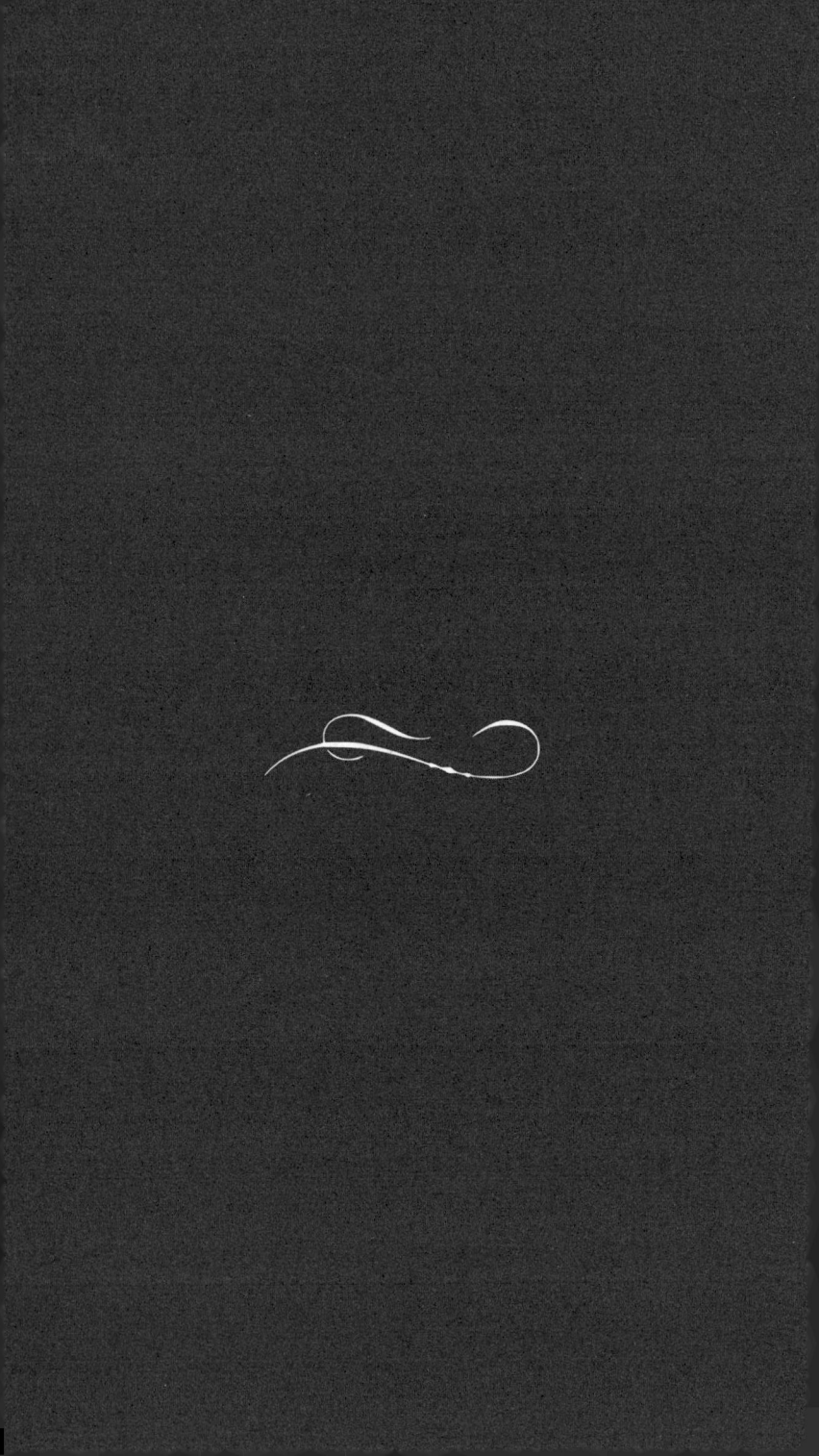

CHAPTER 3

We spent the night in the hotel, and caught the train the next morning. Before leaving, Denton tapped on my door and slipped inside, looking awkward. "Ah . . . I wanted to have a chat with you, if I may?"

"Certainly," I said. I had made an attempt at folding my clothes back into my trunk, which Angus was in the process of correcting. "What's on your mind?"

Denton rubbed the back of his neck. I wondered what made him so ill at ease. You know, other than his cousin vanishing in an abandoned mine full of *squeezes*. "You know that we don't have sworn soldiers here," he said. "I don't know how you want to handle that. I'll do whatever you like, of course."

Oh, is that *all?* I'd already anticipated the issue. What Americans know of Gallacian sworn soldiers derives from the most lurid sort of periodical, where I would likely feature as a six-foot Amazon with a harem of cowed males. (I wouldn't mind being taller, but having a harem of either sex sounds frankly exhausting.) Given the choice between explaining the reality to half the people I met or simply letting them assume that I was a man... no, there was no question. I wasn't thrilled about it, but frankly, I had been tired of explaining matters a decade ago, and by now I had approached a kind of transcendent exhaustion. And what was my other option—wear skirts and let men open doors for me? *No,* thank you. At least when people mistook me for a man, they didn't do anything more obnoxious than demand my opinion of Guam. (To say nothing of the possible dangers if someone decided that I was a woman and thus a potential victim. I did not want to compound the awkwardness of foreign travel by having to shoot someone in the kneecap.)

"It's fine, Denton," I said. "We just won't bother correcting anyone. It's not your fault that your language is so woefully short on pronouns. You don't even have one for talking to God."

"It's an oversight," he admitted. "Alright, then. I'll make sure Ingold knows."

"For a language with so many words in it, it's got some definite flaws," Angus said, once Denton had left.

"I don't know that we get to judge," I said. Gallacian is possibly the most complicated language in Europe. Among its many quirks are different pronouns for men, women, children, soldiers, priests, rocks, and God.

The ones for rocks—sha and shan—don't come up

much, but thinking of Hollow Elk Mine, I had a grim feeling that I might have a use for them sooner rather than later.

The train ride from Boston into West Virginia was extremely long by the standards of Europe, but it was also remarkably comfortable. Denton apologized to us several times for the conditions when we stepped aboard, which was baffling until he explained about Pullman cars and the luxurious accommodations available on some other railways, which apparently included five-star restaurants, barbershops, and all manner of absurdities.

"Is the toilet a board with a hole in it?" I asked, breaking into this monologue after about five minutes.

Denton blinked at me. "God, no!"

"Then it's spectacular. Wake me when we get there."

I settled back in the extremely well-padded seat, pulled my hat down over my eyes, and fell asleep to the sound of Ingold snickering.

The journey took much longer than one nap, as it turned out. I knew intellectually that America was larger than Europe, but when we changed trains and Ingold showed me on a map where Boston was, where the Hollow Elk Mine was, and then exactly how far on that route we had come, I nearly swallowed my teeth. You could have crossed Gallacia three times over in that time, and we hadn't even moved an inch on the map.

Christ's blood. No wonder Americans all move like they've got extra space around them. If their country was a house, it would be one of those monstrous old ramblers that no one can afford to heat in the winter. They probably develop drafts in New York because someone left a window open in San Francisco.

Our fellow passengers were all exuberantly friendly by Gallacian standards. There was a great deal of handshaking, naturally. I only had one bad moment, on one of the platforms when we changed trains, when my tinnitus acted up and the roar of the engine was drowned out by high ringing. A man rushing to meet his train jostled me from behind, and I spun around, suddenly disoriented, expecting the enemy.

My expression must have been alarming, because the man froze like a rabbit, despite being larger than me. What he thought of the short, stocky fellow about to go for his throat, I couldn't guess.

"Steady," said Angus. He must have said it two or three times before the tinnitus faded and reality rushed back, trailing embarrassment in its wake.

"Sorry," I muttered to the man, turning away.

"All right?" asked Denton as we caught up with them.

I shrugged. "Had a moment," I said, a bit gruffly. "Fine now."

Denton nodded and didn't ask any more questions. *Soldier's heart,* they call it here. I'd gotten off lightly, all things considered. There had been those under my command who hadn't been so lucky.

When we finally entered West Virginia the next day, I thought we must be almost there, until Denton gently explained that the state was almost as large as the entire country of Ireland. "So it's a big state?" I asked hopefully.

"Not really, no."

I sank down into the seat and watched the not-very-big state go by. The landscape was spectacular, the hills covered in ranks of trees that blazed the colors of madness, all red and gold and an astonishing shade of pink. And then you'd hit a valley and suddenly everything would be stripped away, the trees toppled, the earth scarred with tracks and great scaffolds of machinery, billows of smoke rising from the pumps that kept the miners from suffocating or drowning or both. And next to that would be a ramshackle little town of a sort I'd seen before, the kind that is kept from being a slum by the sheer willpower of the people who live there.

Then the train would move past and the hills would close over the town and we'd be surrounded by a blaze of trees again.

"So much coal," I muttered as yet another mining town flashed by. "You'd think they'd have enough of it by now."

Ingold snorted. "There's never enough. If people aren't burning it, they're finding new uses for it. That hotel we met at, where everything was purple? That's done with aniline dye made from coal tar."

"You know a lot about this," I said, impressed.

"I'm a chemist. Used to work for DuPont."

"Used to?"

"Decided there were better things to do with my life than finding new ways to dye cloth a slightly different color and then having white men take the credit for it."

I felt a pang of solidarity. I couldn't guess what the situation was like for someone with Ingold's ancestry, but I was certainly used to having men take credit for things. Even when you're a sworn soldier, there's always some jackass who thinks the contents of your pants means you can't possibly be commanding a unit. (As individuals, they're easy enough to deal with, if most of the unit knows you and has your back. If you get a pack of them or, God forbid, a superior officer, things get messy.)

"What do you do now?" I asked.

"I dabble in things." I raised an eyebrow and he laughed. "I dabble in a great *many* things. I read too many papers and tinker with concoctions that mostly no one wants."

"He's being modest," said Denton. "He's a genius."

"I am a singularly unfocused genius." Ingold spread his hands in a self-deprecating manner. "Occasionally I manage to cook up something worth selling. Mostly formulas for dyes. It keeps me out of trouble, more or less."

"Ah." I considered this. "Well, knowing about coal as you do, what do we have to worry about in this mine, other than strange lights? Just the roof falling in?"

"Actually Oscar noted that the timbers were in remarkably good repair, all things considered," Ingold said. "The real problem is likely firedamp. Also black damp, white damp, and stinkdamp."

"That seems like a great many damps."

"Oh yes. Firedamp is what they call methane. It seeps out of the coal and rises. It's extremely flammable and highly explosive." Ingold grinned. "Best of all, it's completely odorless, so we'll have no idea it's there until the shaft explodes."

I edged away from him on the seat.

"Fortunately there's several ventilation shafts, so we may be lucky on that front. And we're using the very best modern safety lamps, which cuts down on the risk of explosions. Then there's black damp, which is heavy and sinks. Fortunately it doesn't explode, it simply smothers you."

". . . fortunately," I said weakly.

"White damp is why miners used canaries, and is probably the most dangerous of the lot. It's left in what's called the afterdamp, after blasting or an explosion. If you begin to feel lightheaded or dizzy, alert someone else immediately." His smile faded. "It can cause hallucinations, and I still think that there's a better-than-even chance that it's behind this entire business." He glanced over at Denton. "If it is, then I don't know if we'll be able to explore the mine safely. It's extremely poisonous. *And* explosive."

"And what was that last one?"

"Stinkdamp. Hydrogen sulfide, smells like rotten eggs. That one, at least, is pretty uncommon."

"Does it explode?" Angus asked, sounding resigned.

"Of course it does," said Ingold, as if surprised that he even had to ask.

I rubbed my temples and wondered if God still looked out for fools, and if so, whether I'd exceeded Har patience already.

Eventually I grew tired of trees and coal towns, so I studied my companions instead of the landscape. There was something just slightly odd about the way they sat on the bench seat, not touching. Ingold, at least, was so pointedly *not* touching Denton that the space between them practically glowed. Which was interesting, and also none of my business. I went back to looking out the window again.

The train chugged on, wheels endlessly repeating their

wordless word. If you listen too long, you can imagine they're saying almost anything. *Dark . . . dark . . . dark. Doom . . . doom . . . doom.*

I scowled, annoyed with myself, and made a conscious effort to map a different word onto the sound. Any word, so long as it wasn't sinister.

Which is why we pulled into the last station with the train wheels chanting *squid . . . squid . . . squid,* because for some reason that was the first word that came to mind.

When we finally got off the train for good, Kent went to arrange for our luggage to be transported, and the rest of us tromped to the livery stable to hire horses. Along the way, we saw the town of Shaversville, although most of the locals called it "Burned Churches," which was a trifle unsettling, and apparently referred to an incident during their civil war. The town consisted of a depot, a mill, a couple of storehouses, a general store, a saloon that doubled as a hotel, a post office that doubled as the telegraph office, and a tangle of shacks that looked to be support for the aforementioned buildings. Also two churches, neither of which looked burned, or even singed.

The livery stable was attached to the hotel. From what I could see, they mostly catered to out-of-towners who came in to work on one of the various local mines. I can't speak to the quality of their accommodations, but I can tell you that quality horseflesh was not a primary concern.

Angus gazed at the five nags presented to us and produced a silence more damning than most men's profanity. I patted my horse on the neck. She gazed past me with an air that reminded me of an elderly Gallacian woman I used to know who had twelve children and twenty-seven grandchildren, and thus no longer registered screaming, crying, wailing, gunshots, explosions, or the sounds of breaking crockery.

On the bright side, she didn't try to shake my hand, which was an improvement over the hostler, who did.

The horses were all equipped with what I am told was a "Western" saddle. Like everything else in America, it was much too large. The horn stuck up so determinedly in front that I couldn't escape the feeling that my saddle was sporting an inconvenient erection, and the minute I leaned down to figure out why the stirrups were so far forward, the horn jabbed me in the gut.

Once we actually started moving, I spent about twenty minutes trying to figure out if the mare was simply ignoring me or if the saddle really was as thick as it felt. It was like riding a couch. A couch with an inconvenient spike in the middle. I tried to imagine what would happen if the mare jumped over something, and had a brief, vivid image of ending my career impaled on a saddle horn in the wilds of West Virginia. Fortunately, I could not imagine this horse jumping without mechanical assistance.

"Are you doing all right?" Ingold called back.

"I'm fine," I said through gritted teeth. I was former cavalry, for God's sake. I was not going to complain to a civilian. (In fairness, I was light cavalry, which mostly meant that we had ridden our horses to the battlefield, then got off to fight, since troops are cheap and horses are expensive. Still. There were principles involved.)

I tried squeezing with my knees. Nothing happened. I shifted my weight. Nothing continued to happen. The mare plodded onward, uninterested in keeping pace with her herdmates.

"You've got to use the reins," said Angus, coming up behind me. "*Just* the reins."

"Like a *barbarian*?" I missed my horse, Hob, with sudden intensity. I could direct Hob with no more than a vague notion that I might like to go in that direction. But he was back in Paris, eating his head off, and I was sliding around like a sack of potatoes on the back of an animal that also rather resembled a walking potato.

Still, it wasn't the mare's fault. I gazed at the reins, sighed, and resigned myself to barbarism.

CHAPTER 4

I don't know what I expected from the entrance to a mine. A big dark hole in the ground, maybe. And indeed, there was a large hole in the side of a hill, but it looked more like the entrance to a train tunnel, assuming the train was about fifty feet wide. It went back about fifty yards, turning into gray twilight inside, with mine cart tracks coming out, but it wasn't the first thing you noticed about Hollow Elk Mine.

No, the first thing was all the *buildings*. There were buildings everywhere, from windowless shacks to a three-story wooden structure directly in front of the mine, and an immense brick chimney at the top of the hillside, the stones blackened with soot. The buildings were in various states of disrepair, ranging from "dilapidated" to "kindling." The big one in front of the mine looked like a couple of barns stacked on top of one another, with sharply angled rooflines and staircases in odd places. (I assume there were chutes or something involved, but I haven't the least idea how coal is mined other than "pickaxe, dynamite, apply one or the other," so don't ask me to explain it.)

We threaded our way past the buildings and stepped into the shadow of the mine entrance. It was a cool autumn day and I was already wearing a coat, but a chill prickled my skin anyway. It felt like entering a cave, and while the sunlight fell bright and crisp behind us, the far wall of the entrance was smothered in shadows.

There was a small building tucked just under the overhang of the tunnel, off to one side, which had been spared the worst of the weathering. It had two rooms and a large window empty of even the memory of glass, which made me suspect that it had been the foreman's office. Judging by the bedroll, the desk, and the scattered papers, it was where Oscar had set up his base of operations.

"There's only one bed," said Angus, frowning.

"Angus, you dog," I said. "I'm flattered, but what will Miss Potter say?"

He rolled his eyes at me. "I *mean* that there were two people staying here, weren't there?"

"Oscar and Roger," Denton agreed. "I didn't think of that when I was here before, but you're right. Roger must have taken his gear and left Oscar's."

"A point in favor of murder?" asked Ingold.

I shrugged. "If I were trying to cover up a murder, I'd take both sets of gear with me, so that it looked like my victim simply left."

Denton grimaced. "We don't know that Roger left after the disappearance," he said. "They may have had a falling out beforehand."

"It's also possible that Oscar was simply lost in the mine, and Roger waited for him until the supplies ran out, then left," Ingold said. Denton's face tightened, but he didn't reply.

Angus had been poking around in the crates and straightened at this. "There's still some tins of food left," he said, holding up a can of peaches. "So he didn't go through them all."

"Perhaps Roger didn't like peaches?" I offered. Angus gave me a look that indicated that this was not a constructive addition to the conversation.

Ingold rubbed his face. "Sadly, I think we don't have enough information yet. We need to find this Roger fellow, if he's still in the area; track down who sent the telegram, if we can; and of course . . ." He waved his hand in the direction of the mine shaft.

I was not looking forward to that bit. Nevertheless, I followed everyone else out of the building and deeper into the hillside.

The gloom increased, the farther back we went. The shaft narrowed down to a line of cart tracks, then angled sharply downward. A jumble of rusted equipment lay off to one side. The shaft had been braced up with timbers as far down as I could see, which wasn't very far at all.

It was very dark and very quiet.

"I suppose we should do this first," said Denton, without much enthusiasm. "At least far enough to make sure that Oscar isn't . . . well . . ." He flicked his fingers, which somehow managed to convey *lying dead at the bottom* without having to actually say it.

"Do we have lights?" I asked. There wasn't much point

in going down if we didn't, and I could just see someone tripping over a discarded pickaxe and breaking their neck.

"The miner's lamps are in the luggage with Kent," said Ingold, "but there's two lanterns back in the foreman's office."

He and Angus went to fetch them. I stood looking down into the dark, with Denton beside me.

It was eerie. No, that understates the case. It was downright *uncanny*, in a way that had nothing to do with ghosts or monsters. You could feel the weight of the stone pressing down overhead, uncounted tons of it, held up by what? A few wooden pillars? Christ's blood, what a ridiculous concept *that* was. As if you could flip a mountain over and hold it suspended by a couple of trees planted on the summit.

Denton had said that what he felt reminded him of the Usher house. I couldn't say that I felt anything like that. Mostly what I felt was an intense belief that humans were not meant to burrow into the earth like worms or moles.

"You didn't go all the way down before?" I asked.

He shook his head, the motion almost invisible in the gloom. "I called for Oscar a few times, but I didn't dare go down on my own. If there's an unexpected drop-off, or if I slid and broke a leg . . ." He trailed off. Thankfully. I imagined lying in pitch blackness at the bottom of the shaft, leg broken, running out of water while the earth pressed down and down and down.

I reminded myself firmly that I was not claustrophobic.

"Dark," I said, unnecessarily.

"Very," Denton replied, equally unnecessarily.

As we stood gazing down, air began to trickle past us with a soft whooshing sound. I took a step back, startled, as the pressure increased. It was only a strong breeze, not difficult to stand against, but it was blowing from behind us, down into the shaft.

"What the devil . . . ?"

The sound rose in pitch to a dull whistle, then the wind began to slacken and it died away.

"Changes in atmospheric pressure," said Denton. "Cave systems breathe the same way. It'll calm down in a bit."

Breathing. That was exactly what it felt like, as if the mine was inhaling, dragging air down a steep stone throat. A throat that had already swallowed one man alive.

If I had been alone, I don't mind telling you that I would have turned around, ridden back to the train station, and gone right back across the ocean to Paris. There may well be mines in France but no one expects me to visit them. I wasn't alone though, and like many fools over the ages, I was determined not to be the one who broke first.

Even the name *Hollow Elk* was troubling. It sounded like an animal gutted and hollowed out, reduced to skin stretched over empty bones. I imagined an elk staggering down the hillside in the dark, hide hanging in tatters. In my mind it moved like the hares from Usher's lake.

I shook my head to clear it. I never used to be this fanciful, or if I was, my fancies were mostly about wine, women, and occasionally, as a distant third, song. Not skinned deer with nothing inside them.

"Why Hollow Elk?" I asked Denton. "Where'd the name come from?"

"Probably from Elk Hollow," he said. "Though around here it would be a *holler*, not a hollow. There's a town called

Banner Elk not far away, so presumably the name of the mine is a take on that."

I liked the idea of a *banner elk* much better, a big sturdy ungulate with flags streaming from its antlers, prancing down the middle of the street during a parade. Why couldn't Denton have inherited a mine like that instead?

Light splashing on the walls around us announced the return of Angus and Ingold, holding lanterns. "We shouldn't go too far down," Ingold said. "If there's a buildup of gas, we don't want to encounter it."

"We'll get loopy?" I asked.

"Our lamps will cause it to explode."

"Oh. Lovely."

Despite this warning, Ingold set off down the shaft without apparent concern. The remaining three of us looked at one another, looked after him, and then followed him into the dark.

The wooden walls of the shaft were dark and uneven, and when I brushed against one, my sleeve came away black with coal dust. The air wasn't noticeably stale, but it wasn't exactly a fresh spring breeze either. Perhaps the mine's breathing wasn't enough to keep it circulating this far down. Mostly it smelled cold and lifeless, as if all the green and growing things aboveground were very far away.

The shaft down was steep but not treacherous. I still wouldn't have wanted to fall down it. We passed several abandoned mine carts and strategically placed wooden backstops, presumably to keep you from tripping and falling all the way to the bottom.

I paid very close attention to my feet because if I looked up, I'd see how low the ceiling was and how puny the timbers were that held up so many thousand weights of stone.

"Here," said Denton, stopping. He held up a lantern and pointed. "That's the first horizontal shaft."

It looked like a black hole in the wall, framed by wooden pillars. We stepped into it one by one. The lantern light might have gone farther if the walls hadn't been black as well.

The tunnel ran back a few dozen yards, then split into three branching tunnels. Denton lifted the lantern higher, and we could just make out where the first tunnel split again.

Bad enough the place is as black as Satan's bowels and there's a mountain on top of you, but it's a maze as well. It's a very good thing I'm not claustrophobic.

"So this damp of yours . . ." I said to Ingold, looking around the shaft. "You said we won't smell it. Could we be standing in it now?"

"Most likely we are," said Ingold, with what I thought was entirely too much enthusiasm. "But not much of it. Wait here just a moment." He walked forward, fingertips skimming the wall, then paused. "Does anyone have a lighter?"

I pulled mine out and handed it over. Ingold flicked it and a spark flashed, and then an eerie blue-white flame appeared on the wall itself, sliding and slithering over a section of stone. A moment later it winked out again.

"*That* was firedamp."

Denton pursed his lips, looking fondly resigned rather than angry. "Could you have exploded the mine, just now?"

"Sure. But I didn't think it was at all likely." Ingold flashed a boyish grin. "The mine's breathing too much, and any firedamp here will rise through the ventilation shafts. It's farther down that we'll really need to worry." He handed my lighter back. "I wouldn't use that anywhere in the mine, though. Just in case."

I shoved my hands into my pockets and told myself that Ingold wouldn't have done that unless he was quite sure it was safe, and therefore my desire to throttle him was entirely unwarranted.

"Is there a map of the tunnels?" asked Angus.

"Not as such," said Denton. "There's an old excavation plan, but it wasn't kept up to date. The third shaft that Oscar wrote about is listed as 'future third shaft,' for example."

Angus made a grumbling noise that managed to indicate his displeasure with the previous ownership of the Hollow Elk Mine.

Denton turned back toward the main shaft. "There's not much point in exploring without headlamps. We'll have to make a map as we go along."

"I'll do the mapping," volunteered Ingold. "As long as somebody else comes with me when I go. I don't mind telling you that I wouldn't want to be down here alone."

There was an almost imperceptible shift in the air as all four of us relaxed a fraction. Someone had said it out loud.

"No, certainly not," said Denton. "No one should go down in the mine alone. Basic safety precautions."

My relief at that pronouncement was almost enough to

get me back to the top of the shaft without the hair on my neck standing on end.

Almost. The mine's breath hissed out, going past us this time, and I was very glad to see the glow of a fire lit outside and to hear Kent informing us that dinner was about to be served.

CHAPTER 5

The next morning, fortunately, the mine was not our first priority. Instead we rode back into town to "make inquiries." Which was fine. I could make inquiries all day if it meant that I was standing in daylight, not gallivanting around at the bottom of a hole.

Once we reached Flatwoods, we split up. Ingold went to find the telegraph office, on the grounds that Ingold could be charming. Denton and Angus went to find Roger, on the grounds that Denton was the only one who would recognize Roger and Angus was good at talking to the salt-of-the-earth mining types, who might balk at talking to Denton.

"You should probably go with Ingold," Angus told me. "Two foreigners nosing around, you'll likely put the wind up their backs."

"Doesn't Boston count as foreign?"

"It's a better quality of foreign, I'm thinking."

I gave that battle up as lost. "I'm not sure that my skills are really much use in a telegraph office."

". . . Your *skills*."

"I have skills, Angus."

"Oh, aye. I've seen 'em. That time in Paris, in the Marais club. Never seen such skills. The gendarmes were verra impressed what you could do with a cocktail onion."

I coughed and went with Ingold.

The telegram office had the look of a new building outfitted with hastily scavenged furniture, the counter old and scarred and smelling faintly of spilled beer. The woman behind the counter was also old and scarred, but smelled faintly of powder instead.

"We wished to inquire about a man who sent a telegram a month ago," said Ingold, with a winning smile.

The clerk was not so easily won. "A month ago," she said flatly. She had glasses on a chain and she pushed them down so that she could look over them at us, an act of aggression to make the stoutest soldier quail. "You expect me to remember a telegram from a *month* ago?"

Ingold looked at me helplessly. I took a deep breath and summoned my best French accent. "Mademoiselle," I said, with all the old-world charm that I could muster, "I expect that you have forgotten more than my friend and I have ever learned. But may I trouble you to look at the telegram, s'il vous plaît? My friend is very concerned, and it may help us greatly."

"Hmmm." She surveyed me over the glasses, clearly skeptical. I tried to look French, which isn't easy when you are covered in dust. (A proper Frenchman can make dust look exquisite. Mind you, a proper Frenchman would have died of despair at my accent.) Nevertheless, she pushed her glasses back up and extended her hand. "All right, show me."

Ingold handed her the telegram. She unfolded it, scanned it for barely a second, and gave a short laugh. "Oh, *him*! I'm not likely to forget that fellow."

I put my elbows on the counter, ignoring the scent of beer. "Please, Mademoiselle, I am all ears."

"Tall fellow," she said, placing the telegram on the counter. "Wore dark goggles like a miner, right into the office. And he didn't talk none, either."

"Didn't talk?"

She shook her head. "Wrote out what he wanted to send. Had a bit of slate and chalk. Told him it was going to be expensive, sending a whole long message like this, but he didn't care. Just shoved a whole pocketful of money at me, and left with never a word."

"Huh," I said.

"Huh," Ingold said.

We stood outside the telegraph office, blinking in the bright sunlight. I wasn't sure if we'd learned something vital or not. The miner's helmet and goggles had apparently covered most of the man's face, and no amount of French would convince the clerk to describe his jawline and the tip of his nose.

"Do you think it was Oscar?"

Ingold made a helpless gesture. "No idea. But I agree with Denton that Roger couldn't have written that telegram."

I suppressed a sigh. I hadn't really been hoping that the clerk would say, "Oh, the telegram was sent by so-and-so, you know, the one who murdered that Oscar fellow," but it would have been nice.

For lack of anything better to do, we went over to the hotel bar—or perhaps it was a saloon, I'm not clear on the difference—and had a beer while we waited.

"So how did you meet Denton?" I asked.

Ingold grinned. "He lived upstairs from me. Still does, actually. We passed in the hall more often than not, until one day one of my experiments got a trifle . . . ah . . . exciting."

I raised my eyebrows. "It exploded?"

"No, no, nothing *that* dramatic. Produced a quantity of noxious gas. Probably not fatal, but I thought it was my civic duty to go up and warn him to open the windows. He was really very nice about the whole thing."

This fit with my experience of Denton as an affable soul. I could practically hear him sigh heavily as he threw open the windows.

"At any rate, he asked what I was doing, and I offered to show him, and we became—ah—friends. Lovely chap." He took a sip of his beer.

The "lovely chap" had been a little too casual. I was developing a suspicion about what that friendship entailed, but it continued to be none of my business.

Ingold cocked an eye in my direction. "He told me how he met you. I suspect you might tell the story differently."

I leaned back in the chair. "Oh, I don't know about that. Although anything he says about me hiding in the library is a filthy lie."

Ingold smiled. "He said you were as brave as a lion."

"Well. Denton was no slouch himself." I took a hasty swig of beer. You shouldn't just spring earnest praise on a person like that. It's embarrassing.

Fortunately, at that moment, the door opened and Angus and Denton breezed in.

"Good news," Denton said. "Hopefully. We've found Roger."

I'm not certain what to call the cluster of shacks outside of Flatwoods. *Slum* seems overly harsh, and *ghetto* implies a city, which Flatwoods wasn't. This was a cluster of run-down shacks, the remains of a company town from another failed mining venture. Everything of use to the company had been stripped out, leaving dozens of small, weathered buildings that leaned together at odd angles, as if for warmth.

A man came out to meet us as the four of us rode up, looking both official and suspicious. "Can I help you gents?" he asked. He was a tall Black man with a battered stovepipe hat. I could see a nervous-looking woman watching from the doorway of his house. It was a pose that I was intimately familiar with. Every time you ride into a village that's been newly taken or retaken from the enemy, people watch you from doorways like that, wondering if you're there to do something violent.

I hadn't been expecting to see it in the middle of America, which was thirty years past any local wars. I draped my hands over the saddle horn and tried to look harmless.

"We're looking for a man named Roger Clement," said

Denton, sliding down from his horse so that he could address the man face-to-face. "We're not here to make any trouble for anybody, just looking for my cousin."

Stovepipe's eyebrows went up. "Roger's your cousin?"

"No, no. He works for my cousin. Well, he used to, anyway." Denton put up his hands placatingly. "Just wanted to ask him a few questions."

I winced internally at that. Probably there's a culture where *ask him a few questions* isn't a euphemism for *beat him until answers fall out,* but I've yet to encounter it.

Stovepipe pretty clearly knew both meanings of the phrase. His eyes were shuttered. I slid off my mare and approached, wearing my best "talking to civilians" expression of good-natured concern.

"Do you know Roger?" I asked. "Is he doing all right? Hasn't been hurt, has he?"

Stovepipe looked me over, then grunted. "He's dead drunk most of the time," he said, "but I ain't seen any blood on him. And he hasn't run afoul of—" He stopped, clearly deciding that we didn't need to know how that sentence ended. "Why?"

I was very curious what we didn't need to know, but this wasn't the moment to press him. "His cousin's gone missing," I said, nodding to Denton, "and the family's worried something's happened to him. Roger was his best friend. We're just trying to figure out what happened before his aunt"—I jerked my chin at Denton—"has a nervous breakdown and takes it out on the rest of the family."

"It's more than my life's worth to go back to Boston without some kind of news," said Denton. "Aunt Lydia'll box my ears so hard that my grandfather will feel it."

That got a half smile out of Stovepipe. "Up the hill. Last building on the left." I don't know if he believed us or if he had decided that Roger wasn't worth defending against four people. Either way, his role as de facto peacekeeper of the community seemed satisfied.

"Thank you kindly," I said, and tossed him a coin. I couldn't remember what the denomination was, but he caught it and didn't look insulted, so probably it was fine.

We led the horses up the hill, toward the last building on the left. "Thanks," murmured Denton. "Seemed like he was expecting trouble."

"I'm guessing not too many people come out here for social calls."

Roger's shack was leaning drunkenly against the hillside and a couple of timbers had been shoved in place to brace it there. The front door—well, the only door—was open, and a big black dog lay across the doorway. It appeared to be asleep.

"Roger?" called Denton.

The dog opened its eyes and stood up. I revised my estimate of its size upward from *big* to *huge.* It looked at us and made a hoarse coughing noise that sounded like a bear attempting to bark.

From inside the shack, I heard a noise somewhere between a "Huh?" and a snore.

"Roger? Are you in there?"

The dog barked again. Someone—presumably Roger—said, "What? Who's askin'?"

"It's Denton, Oscar's cousin."

Thumping. More barking. The grunt of someone sitting up, against long odds. "Mister Oscar? Didja find him?"

My heart sank. If we were looking for an easy solution to the mystery, it seemed to have gone by the wayside.

"Get outta the way, Thunder," Roger said, and the dog sagged back down. Roger appeared behind him, shirtless, with a scraggly growth of beard and the bleary eyes of someone who was on the wrong end of a hangover.

"We're looking for Oscar," Denton said. "May we come in?"

"Oh." Roger slumped. He was wiry rather than big, and with his shoulders bowed, he looked small and sick and old before his time. Not someone I'd have hired to work for me. I wondered what the absent Oscar had seen in him.

"Yeah, you can come in," said Roger. He nudged Thunder with his foot, which did exactly nothing.

The shack was exactly what you'd expect it to be—small, dirty, filled with empty bottles. It smelled like old sweat and despair. Denton went in. I stayed in the doorway, looking at the dog.

Now, most of us, when we see a dog, think, *Yay! A dog! Can I pet it?* We do not think, "Hmm, a large predator capable of tearing my throat out in an instant." This dog, however . . . I rubbed my neck, wishing I had a scarf, or perhaps plate mail.

"Can you tell me where you last saw him?" Denton asked.

"Sure. He went into that damn mine again and didn't come out. I told him not to." Roger sat down on the bed, his face in his hands. "I *told* him it was bad." He sounded on the edge of tears and I revised my opinion from "hungover" to "still a little drunk."

Despite my better judgment, I crouched down and offered Thunder my fingertips to sniff. The dog's nose didn't so much as twitch. He stared at me instead. It was unsettling.

"Did you look for him?" Denton asked.

"Course I looked for him! I went all over that damn place looking! But he must've gone down deep and there's too much there. Couldn't possibly check it all." Roger looked away while he said it, and I suspected that, however much he'd loved Oscar, he hadn't spent very long looking "down deep."

"Do you think he got lost down there?" asked Denton.

Thunder continued his unblinking stare.

"Lost. Maybe."

"You don't sound convinced."

"There's bad stuff down deep. I told him not to go down there."

I realized that I was now in a staring contest with a dog and looked away to prove that I was the more intelligent species. When I checked out of the corner of my eye, he was still staring.

"What sort of bad stuff?"

Roger rolled his eyes and looked over at me, as if to say, *Is this man dim?* "If I knew what it was, I wouldn't just say 'bad stuff,' now would I?"

Denton tried another tactic. "Oscar wrote to me to say that somebody was stealing supplies and he found some of them in the mine. Do you think that person might have had something to do with it?"

"Wasn't a person," Roger said.

"It wasn't?"

"Nah. Thunder would've had something to say if somebody was sneaking around, wouldn't you, boy?"

The dog finally turned his head toward Roger, but I don't think he stopped watching me.

"That's why I ain't worried about the bear or whatever it is out there," Roger said, gesturing toward the world outside.

"Bear?" I asked, curious.

"They say it's a bear. I dunno. Killed a couple of pigs and then did for old Asa. Tore his liver and lights right out and ate 'em. Everybody's spooked, but I ain't. Not with Thunder around. Best damn watchdog in the state."

Looking at Thunder, I could quite see his point. Any bear encountering Thunder would probably apologize and ask for directions to the nearest road out of town.

"Could a bear have gotten Oscar?" asked Denton.

"Ain't no bears in the mine, chief. And anyway, this one didn't show up until recent like."

Denton asked him a few more questions, trying to nail down the exact day that Oscar had vanished, and how long before Roger had given up and left. Roger answered, although his recollections were hazy now. He kept glancing toward the bottle on the table next to him and it was easy to see that he was waiting for us to leave so that he could start drinking again.

Denton promised to be in touch and gave Roger five dollars to thank him for taking the time to talk to us. Thunder watched us leave with frightening intensity.

We had remounted the horses when Roger appeared in the doorway. "Hey, doc."

"Yes?"

"You oughta stay out of that mine. But I don't figure you're going to, so I'll tell you this. You want to know what happened to Mr. Oscar, you look for a red light. That's how you find whatever's down there. That damn red light."

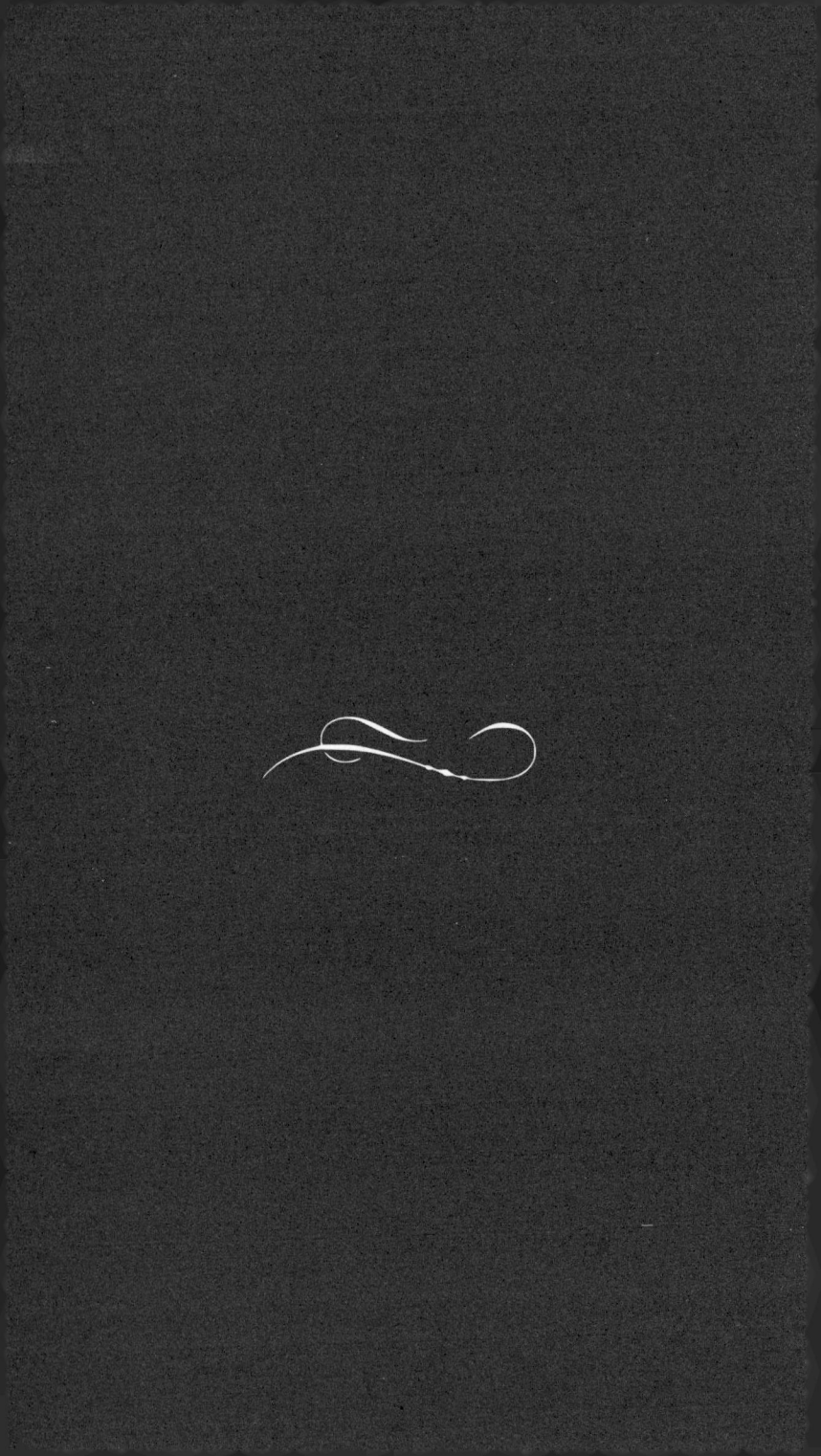

CHAPTER 6

Upon returning to the mine that evening, we discovered that Kent had finished making camp, in much the same sense that an army makes camp when it settles in for the duration. He had set up a kitchen area and dishwashing station, improved the picketing for the horses, and spruced up the latrine. I can't swear to it, but I think he even fluffed my pillow.

"Well," I said as we ate the surprisingly good meal that Kent had produced out of tins over an open fire. "What's next?"

I knew the answer of course. We'd found Roger, and we had no idea where to find the man who had sent the telegram. That left only one avenue to explore, and it was lying beneath our feet.

Given the size of the mine, we determined—or rather, Denton determined, and we all agreed—that we should start by mapping the third horizontal shaft, the deep one that Oscar had described in his letters. If something had happened to him in the mine, his body was most likely down there, not in one of the upper levels.

"And I'm curious about this pearl chamber he wrote about," said Ingold. "It must be a natural formation, but I'm stumped as to what it could be. There are cave systems all through West Virginia, but none that I'd describe as pearl."

I was beginning to understand Ingold, and I confess, I found him rather charming. He was, above all, *interested* in things. He wanted to know why things worked, but unlike some scientific minds, he didn't lose interest once he knew. The world was an endless source of fascination and wonder. On our way back from town, he whipped out a magnifying lens to show me what he called a "wheel bug"—a bizarre insect with a thick body and tiny head, and a strange ridge on its back. "Look at him!" Ingold said, clearly delighted. "Or her, I suppose—I can't tell them apart."

"Presumably they know." The bug had a small, wickedly sharp pointy bit tucked under its absurdly small head. "What do they eat?"

"Other bugs. They're a member of the assassin bug clan. They drive that beak into an insect and pump it full of digestive juices until its innards turn to liquid, then slurp it all back out."

I took a step back from the wheel bug, even though it seemed extremely unconcerned about our existence or its current place in the spotlight. "That sounds painful."

"Excruciating, I should imagine. If one stabs you, it hurts like a sonuvabitch, so don't put your hand on one." He beamed at me, putting his lens away. "They're slow and docile and not terribly bright and if you underestimate them, they extract a terribly painful vengeance. Isn't that marvelous?"

I agreed that it was. It came as no surprise that Ingold was as eager to see this pearl chamber as Denton was to find out what had happened to his cousin.

For my part, I could have left at once and the mystery would have nagged at me for perhaps ten minutes total, but I am, as I have said before, a simple soul. Leaving Denton to face the unknown alone, though, would have eaten at me for the rest of my life.

Bright and early in the morning, therefore, Ingold assembled his mapping equipment—a compass, a notebook, and a long string—and looked for a partner to spot him in the depths of the mine. I could think of nothing that I would like less, so naturally I volunteered. (If this doesn't make sense to you then I suggest you reflect for a time on the Spanish word *macho,* and on how even sworn soldiers who damn well ought to know better still occasionally find themselves with something to prove. Besides, I wasn't claustrophobic.)

The mine had not improved in the last forty-eight hours. The weight of it still hung over me like the sword of Damocles, although swords are light and thin and airy, so perhaps this was more like the club of Damocles. *The maul of Damocles. The bloody huge rock of Damocles . . .*

We descended the shaft to the third horizontal tunnel, and paused. The main shaft kept going downward. "Should we go all the way down?" I asked, hoping that Ingold would say no.

"At least to make certain there's not another tunnel we missed," said Ingold, and down we went.

I couldn't say how much farther we went. Not terribly far, I think, but my perceptions were definitely being colored by my surroundings. I could *hear* things. Little noises, like distant sighs, and the occasional creak, like an old house settling. Things you wouldn't think twice about aboveground.

It's just the mine breathing, I told myself. *There's no one else here.*

No one alive, anyway.

That wasn't a comforting thought. I don't *disbelieve* in ghosts, but that's not quite the same thing as believing in them. I have no reason to believe that the spiritualists were lying. I had encountered ... something ... in Gallacia that I still could not quite pass off as a hallucination brought on by fever. (It is possible that I believe in ghosts less now than I did before, because if I admit that they are real, I will have to admit that what happened to me was also real and that I killed a lost, starving ghost in a dream of a war that never ends.)

In the depths of the Hollow Elk Mine, though, it was easier to believe. Not in ghosts precisely, but in things that did not follow nature's laws as I understood them. Hollow Elk did not feel haunted. It felt *alien*.

The blackness at the edge of our headlamps became deeper and flatter and then the smell changed to something dank and oily and we found ourselves looking down at a pool of water the color of tar.

"Well, that's that then," said Ingold. "I suppose if this mine was still active, they'd use pumps."

I stared at the water. It was absolutely flat and looked

poisonous. "Is there a chance that Denton's cousin is in there?"

Ingold grimaced. The beam from his headlamp jerked across the tunnel walls as he turned toward me. "If he is, we're not going to find him. That water's more acidic than vinegar, and full of arsenic. You don't want to go mucking about in it."

In this, he was absolutely correct. I took a few more steps forward anyway, playing my headlamp over the water's edge, just in case there was . . . oh . . . a hand lying half out of the pool or something.

"Easton, wait," said Ingold from behind me. "Back up."

I obeyed hurriedly. When a man who sets firedamp alight tells you to back up, you don't argue.

"Farther," he said, waving me behind him. "This is where blackdamp would be. Let's check."

Another damp. Lovely. "Does this one explode?"

"No, quite the opposite." Ingold pulled a candle from his pack and lit it. Pulling his shirt up over his nose and mouth, he inched down the slope, holding the candle in front of him.

He was only a step or two farther along than I had been when the flame winked out. He scrambled back up, looking pleased with himself. "As I thought. Blackdamp is heavy, so it gathers in the low places."

I winced. "And what would that do to us?"

"Oh, you'll suffocate," he said. "You'd feel lightheaded and fatigued first, mind you. Then it hits a critical level and . . ." He mimed a swoon.

"I suppose that's better than being splattered all over the landscape."

"Really?" Ingold looked thoughtful. "I think I'd rather be splattered. It's much more dramatic, don't you think?"

"I've seen more than my share of dramatic deaths," I said, perhaps a bit more testily than Ingold deserved.

He stopped in his tracks, and since I was following him, I stopped, too.

"I'm sorry," he said. "That was thoughtless of me. You and Denton both, I should know better." Ingold shook his head. "And now I'm drawing attention to it, which is probably worse. Sorry again."

"It's all right," I said. "Things are what they are." It was kind of him to acknowledge it anyway, and to be aware that even the acknowledgment was fraught.

We ascended back to the third tunnel and Ingold took out his notebook and began to draw.

The mine wasn't a maze, fortunately. Each tunnel split off into others, usually two or three, spread out like fans, but finding your way back to the main shaft was easy enough. All that you had to do was turn around and take the passage back to where it met up with others, then take the passage opposite the branch, over and over, until you were back at the root. Nevertheless, each of those passages had to be mapped, and Ingold carefully paced each one, paced it again to confirm, then noted the numbers down in his book.

That boredom and terror are bedfellows is of no surprise to any soldier. Watching Ingold rapidly stopped being interesting, while the darkness continued to press down on us like physical weight. I had a bad moment when we reached a dead end and Ingold pointed out a hole that had been hollowed out under the stone wall and explained that a miner would lie down there, wedged tightly beneath the rock, and pick away until there was enough space to blast out with explosives. Just imagining being stretched out with the stone *right there* at your back was enough to make the six inches of air currently between my head and the ceiling seem as holy as the air inside any Gallacian cathedral.

I've no idea how many tunnels Ingold had carefully plotted when I started to hear the echo.

Our footsteps echoed, of course. There was no way that they wouldn't. After a time, we stopped paying attention, or perhaps I would have noticed it sooner. But gradually I noticed that when Ingold was pacing out his latest tunnel, there was an echo that did not seem quite right. It went on an instant too long and it fell flat instead of ringing. And it sounded . . .

. . . wet.

My ears pricked up and I pushed myself away from the wall I'd been leaning on, listening. For a moment there was nothing, then Ingold paced by again and I caught the sound, just at the edge of my hearing, a quiet slap like a damp towel dropped onto a stone floor.

Your ears are playing tricks on you, old fellow, that's all. It's this place.

That was almost certainly the case, but I kept listening anyway, and heard it again and again. Soft and wet and somehow *sly* in the way that it stopped as soon as we stopped, and did not start again until we did. Nothing at all like a human footstep.

And it seemed to be between us and the main shaft.

Under the pretext of looking over Ingold's shoulder

at the map, I whispered, "Don't say anything, but I think there's something following us. Listen for a wet slapping sound."

"Yes," said Ingold, a little too loudly, "it's coming along well, I think." He stood up, giving me a wide-eyed look, and I remembered that he was a civilian. I led the way forward, then stopped abruptly, and there it was again, that soft wet sound, caught out in mid-motion.

What the hell would make a sound like that?

I was pretty sure it had to be intelligent, whatever it was, or it wouldn't have been trying to hide the sound of its movements. But intelligent like a stalking cat, or intelligent like a human being?

Firing a gun inside a mine seemed like a terrible idea, between Ingold's firedamp and the chance of the ceiling coming down on us. Nevertheless, I wished desperately that my pistol wasn't with my other gear at the top of the shaft.

"Perhaps it's time we go back," I said aloud.

"Certainly," Ingold said. "I need to compile these notes anyway."

We turned around and started walking.

Slap . . . slap . . . slap . . .

It was ahead of us now. Between us and the exit. Christ's blood. It was still moving, though, and I hoped like hell that it was retreating from us.

We reached a point where three tunnels merged into the main one. We had only mapped the leftmost of the three. Had it gone into the main tunnel? Was it waiting to attack or trying to get away from us in hopes of remaining unseen?

It had plenty of chances to attack you while your backs were turned, and even while you were a dozen yards apart and nicely split up.

If it was trying to get away, I wanted to give it plenty of opportunities. "Let's check this one tunnel," I told Ingold, and went down the right-hand passageway, mostly at random.

I regretted my choice almost immediately. The tunnel narrowed down until our heads brushed the ceiling, then farther yet. I paused, listening hard, but couldn't hear any slapping noises. It wasn't following us.

Maybe it doesn't plan to attack us.

Or maybe it went back for reinforcements.

"It didn't follow us in," I whispered to Ingold. "But I don't want it between us and the shaft, so I'm giving it time to get out of the way."

Ingold nodded. He went past me, first hunching over, then practically bending double. I reminded myself just how claustrophobic I wasn't and followed.

"Did they not excavate this far?" I asked.

"That's not it," he said. "Here, it opens up ahead."

"Oh thank God," I muttered in Gallacian. Sure enough, a few yards up, the ceiling rose and we could stand normally.

"That was a squeeze," said Ingold.

My stomach clenched around the word. "Is sha going to fall on us?"

"Sha?"

"It's what we call rocks instead of *it*."

"Really? How interesting. Is it just rocks? Or would the tunnel also be sha?"

"No, tunnels are *it*, but they're made of rocks, which are *shan*." I felt lightheaded and the conversation wasn't helping much. "Maybe this isn't the time for comparing languages." I took a few deep breaths, trying to steady my nerves, but it didn't help. The air felt stale and thick. When I turned, the walls kept turning a little too long without me, as if I was drunk.

Ingold frowned at me. "Are you alright?"

"I'm fine," I lied. "Just tense."

His eyes narrowed. "No," he said. "No, I don't think you are."

"Believe me," I said grimly, "I am *definitely* tense."

"Yes, yes. Not that." He waved a hand. "Do you feel queasy?"

I opened my mouth to deny it, but my stomach hadn't unclenched at all. "I suppose? A little?"

"Firedamp," said Ingold grimly. "We're standing in a pocket of it. We have to go back."

"Oh," I said. I felt somewhat pleased by this revelation. *See, I'm not claustrophobic. The squeeze was nothing. It's the mine gas that's killing me, that's all.*

"*Now*, Alex," said Ingold.

I fired off a salute, spun in place, watched the walls spin on without me, and staggered sideways.

It's just like being drunk, I told myself. *You understand being drunk. You have been epically, amazingly heroically drunk before. Remember that time in Greece?*

Ingold was pulling at my arm for some reason. Did he want my coat? He could just ask. Nevertheless it was awfully hot, so I began trying to take my coat off, but that didn't seem to satisfy him. He grabbed my shoulder and pushed my head down toward the floor, which isn't behavior that I tolerate from anyone, friend or not.

I attempted to explain this to him but he did not seem to be paying attention. Instead he shoved me into the wall. No, not the wall, the tunnel. Unless the wall had opened up at the bottom? Tricky wall.

A light zipped crazily from wall to floor and back again. Ingold was still pawing at me. Obviously he was drunker than I was. I was going to have to take a swing at him in a moment if he didn't stop.

He shoved me again, hard. I lost my footing and went to my knees. Then someone bellowed, "*Forward!*" and that meant *march*, or at least *crawl*, an order which bypassed my brain entirely. I crawled. The light kept wobbling around in front of me like it was drunk, too.

We were well past the squeeze before I realized that it was my own headlamp making the zigzagging light. A minute later I realized that I was *not* drunk, and a minute after that, Ingold said, "That's probably far enough."

"Ah," I said, after a long few minutes. The walls were stable again and I could stand up, which I did, cautiously. "We nearly died just then, didn't we?"

"I believe so." Ingold mopped at his forehead. "I've poisoned myself in the lab once or twice, but it usually took a lot longer."

Everyone handles a brush with death differently. I have a system where I think, *Christ's blood, I nearly died!* until my body finally catches up with my brain. Then I have the cold shakes for a few minutes. Then I stare off into space for a few minutes. Staring off into space in a mine is quite dull though, so when Ingold suggested we go back up to camp, I agreed.

By that point, I also felt well enough to be embarrassed. "Sorry about that," I muttered.

Ingold shook his head. "Not your fault. It's mine gas, not a personal failing."

Which was true, but still, I was the one who had succumbed, not him. He'd had the sense to shove me out of the gas, while I was still spinning in place.

"Yeah, let's go back up," I said. I hadn't heard any wet slapping for some time, but that might just have meant that whatever it was knew about the firedamp. Which wasn't a particularly happy thought, so I put it on the pile of other unhappy thoughts that I'd been having since we reached Hollow Elk Mine.

Still, as we followed the main tunnels back to the shaft, I strained my ears and heard nothing but our own footsteps. Whatever had been shadowing us was gone.

I smelled ham cooking before we were far enough up the shaft to see firelight. Kent had set up the campfire in the mouth of the mine entrance, and I was very glad to drop down next to it and pretend my hands weren't shaking. Night had fallen while we were down there, not that day and night matter much underground.

"A wet slapping noise?" asked Denton, when we finished recounting the details. "Are you sure it wasn't water dripping?"

"Very sure," I said, warming my hands by the fire. The adrenaline was wearing off, but my hands always stay cold for a bit after a brush with death. I wished that my horse, Hob, was here. I could have gone and shoved my face against his neck until I felt better. But the horses were picketed in full view of the cave entrance, and anyway, I doubted the mare would have appreciated it.

"Oscar talked about a squelching in his letter," Denton said. "Do you think it's the same thing?"

I shrugged helplessly. "Maybe? How many words does English have for a weird wet noise?"

"I think it was probably the same," Ingold put in. "And it wasn't mine gas, because we both heard it. There's definitely something down there, and it followed us for a good distance."

Denton pinched the bridge of his nose. "Dammit," he muttered. "I really hoped I was wrong about all of this."

"If it helps any, so did I," I said.

He was all for leaving at once to try to track down the source of the sound, but Ingold put his foot down. "Let us get a little more air in us before we go haring off again." (It was kind of him to say *us*, since I suspected that I'd been knocked down much harder by the firedamp than he had.) Denton agreed, grudgingly, but kept looking over his shoulder at the entrance to the shaft. Soldiers look like that when they *know* their comrades are dead, but they can't shake the urgent sense that if they just go back out soon enough, maybe a miracle will be waiting.

Kent, who could cook a three-course meal over a campfire, announced that dinner was served. I took my tin plate of beans, ham, and biscuits and dug in.

"On the bright side," said Angus, sitting down beside me, "at least this means we didn't waste a boat ride."

Denton was on his feet as soon as our plates were empty. I really didn't want to go back down, which of course is why I did it. We have a saying in Gallacia: "When the wolf bites your heart, don't wait for him to shit," which means, "If you're scared of doing something, don't put it off." (Ingold tells me there's a similar American saying about getting back on a horse.) The longer I waited to go back down, the more I'd keep reliving drowning in mine gas, and the worse it was going to be.

The wolf's teeth were firmly in place as we made our way back down to the third shaft. We gave the squeeze a wide berth and returned to the tunnels where we'd heard the strange wet sound, and began to go back and forth, listening. I felt like an ant moving in the darkness of an anthill. Do individual ants ever think about the earth over their heads and feel uneasy?

If so, I bet they don't tell the other ants about it.

It would have been nice, since I was being quietly stoic, to be rewarded by hearing the ... whatever it was ... but we walked around for the better part of an hour without hearing anything more alarming than the creaks and groans of an old mine. (Which are quite alarming enough, thank you.)

"Are you sure this was where you heard it?" Denton asked.

"Absolutely," said Ingold.

Denton didn't ask again, and he didn't ask if we were sure we *had* heard it, which perversely made me less certain than I had been. If I'd had to argue that there had been a sound, I would have convinced myself thoroughly, but now I began second-guessing everything. Could it have been a strange echo? Some drip into the poisoned lake at the bottom of the shaft? Some whiff of mine gas turning both our heads?

"We can try again tomorrow," Ingold said finally. "It's getting late."

I didn't need any encouragement to turn back toward the main shaft. Denton lagged behind us, still listening. I glanced over my shoulder, worried about leaving him behind, when he stopped dead, yanked off his helmet, and hissed, "Turn off your lamps!"

Years of worrying about a careless cigarette giving away our position to the enemy snapped into place. I had my lamp off and extinguished in seconds. Ingold, perhaps unwilling to be stranded completely in the dark, turned his light to point away from Denton. "What—" he started to say, and then he stopped.

Far down the tunnel, a spark of red burned against the darkness.

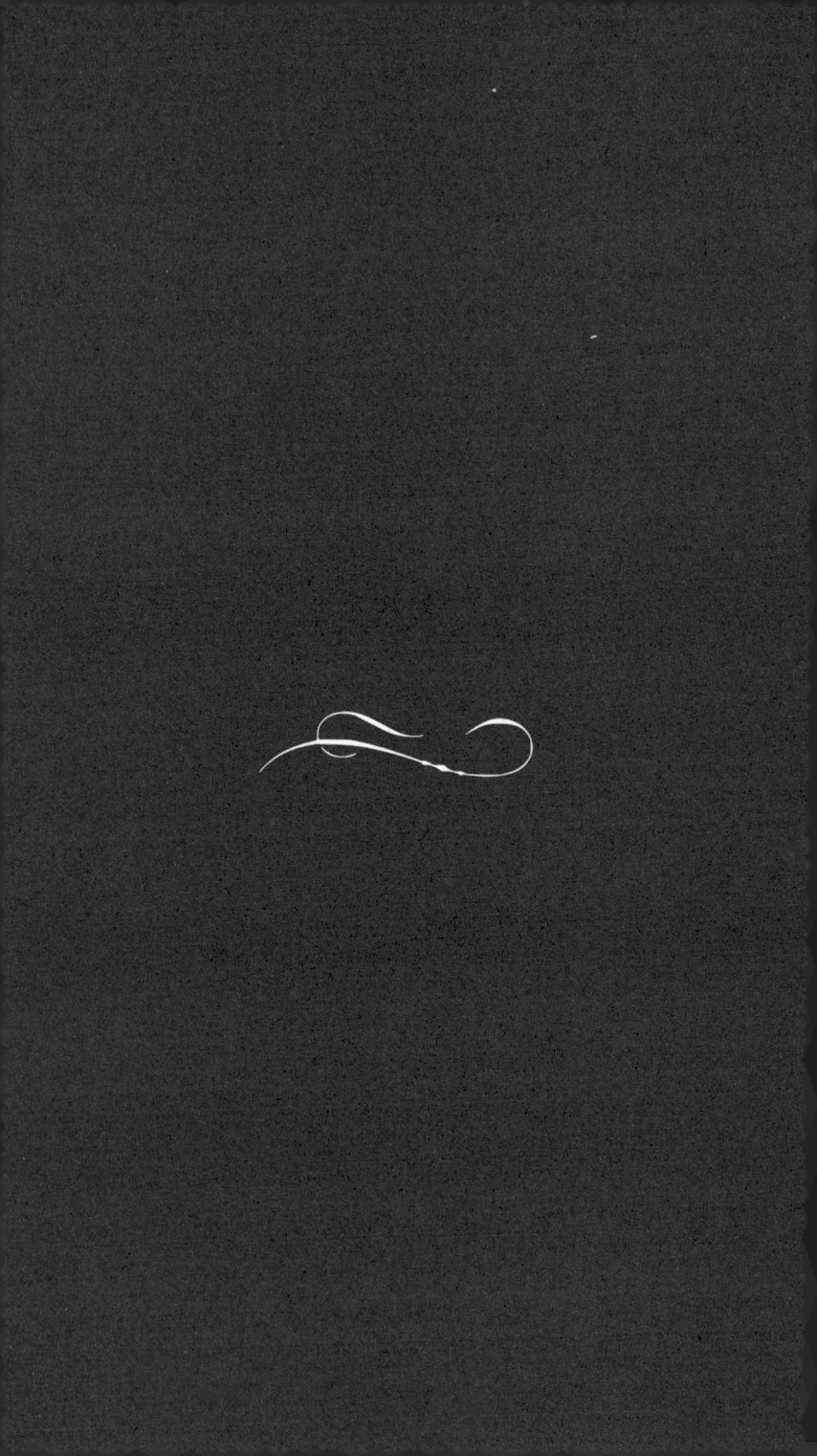

CHAPTER 7

There are many reasons not to run in a dark mine, and Denton presumably thought of them, because he cursed softly, then whispered, "Can you point your lamp down?"

Ingold did. I left mine off. We crept forward in the gloom, alternating between watching our feet and looking up to see if the red light was still there. It was hard to tell at first, since it was the same dull red color as the afterimages that burn onto your eyes. I kept staring at it for too long, half-convinced that my eyes were playing tricks on me, then stumbling over the uneven floor.

As our eyes adjusted though, the light came into better focus. It was an unmoving glow, not like our headlamps, but without the flicker of firelight. Irregular shadows loomed against it, coming clearer as we approached. A rockfall, possibly, or just a pile of debris left over from excavation. It was hard to tell how far away it was. Farther than I thought initially, anyhow. Tunnels branched off to our right, but we kept inching forward, drawn by the bloody red light.

"This is what Oscar wrote about," Denton breathed. His whisper sounded as loud as a scream in my ears.

I had to swallow twice before my mouth would form the words, "Must be."

After long minutes of not getting any closer to the rockfall, suddenly it was right in front of us. It was chest-high, with only a narrow gap at the top. Anyone wriggling through would be vulnerable to an attacker waiting on the other side. Ingold flicked the edge of the light along the scarred ceiling, then lowered it to the ground again.

"Was it a cave-in?" I whispered.

"Looks like it."

I closed my eyes briefly. "Gas?"

"Doesn't look angled to trap it, no."

"Good enough," Denton murmured, and set his foot on the rubble. Rocks rolled and clattered together under his boot, loud as a gunshot in the silent belly of the mine.

The red light went out.

Denton cursed. Ingold whipped his light back around, the beam nearly blinding me. Blood-rainbows danced in front of my eyes, and then we heard it—a flurry of wet slapping sounds, right on the other side of the cave-in, no longer stealthy but rapid, like a fish dragged out onto land and beating itself against stone.

The sounds reached a crescendo, mere feet away, and then suddenly they were moving away, into the distance, and then . . . gone.

Denton was already at the top of the rubble pile, scrambling through the crawl space. Ingold was close behind him. I took a moment to turn my lamp back on, telling myself that it was only sensible and certainly not because I wanted someone *else* to find out if there was firedamp on the far side before I jammed myself into a narrow death trap on the arse-end of a mountain. Then I cursed myself for cowardice and started up the pile.

My head scraped the ceiling at the narrowest point, then my back. I had an image of getting jammed between the stone and the rock, knees against my chest, unable to move forward or back... *Christ's blood.* I went flat and hauled myself forward like a worm in a panic.

I heard Denton saying, "What the devil...?" as I clambered over the loose rock and pitched headfirst into the space beyond.

For a moment, I was busy trying to breathe and convince my nerves that I had *not* gotten stuck and the air I was breathing was *not* firedamp. Eventually my nerves decided to accept this as a polite fiction and I could focus on what Ingold and Denton were staring at.

Which looked an awful lot like a body in miner's clothes.

Strangely, this helped settle my nerves. Mines are enemy territory for me, but I have experience with all kinds of bodies. "Dead?" I asked.

"Never alive," said Ingold. He flipped one empty sleeve at me. (Well, it *had* looked awfully flat, come to think of it.)

Sure enough, what I'd taken for a body was a set of miner's clothing—trousers, shirt, socks, boots, all laid out on the floor, facedown and arms spread. A miner's helmet and goggles topped the set, the headlamp unlit.

"Strange place to leave your clothes," Denton said.

"Strange *way* to leave your clothes," Ingold said. "They

buttoned everything back up and then laid it out on the ground like this."

There was something oddly unsettling about the fact that it was facedown. I'm not sure why that struck me more than anything, but it just seemed so peculiar. If you're laying out clothes for later, you lay them out faceup. (You also don't leave them in the middle of a collapsing mineshaft God knows how deep underground, but that's neither here nor there.)

I looked down the tunnel and saw at once why Denton hadn't continued his pursuit of the red light. The passage continued perhaps twenty feet, then ended in another wall of rubble. This one was even higher than the last, with perhaps a foot of clearance at the top. Irregular chunks of stone lay scattered along the floor, some of them nearly the size of my head. This was looking more and more like the site of a cave-in, which did not exactly fill me with confidence.

"Well," said Denton, playing his lamp along the narrow gap. "Whatever it was must have been smaller than it sounded."

"I suppose it might have been a frog," I said, without much conviction.

"At the bottom of a mine? Glowing red?"

"I don't know, maybe you have strange American glow-frogs here."

"I believe those are limited to Australia," said Ingold, deadpan.

Denton shook his head. "We'll have to move these rocks and see what's on the other side." He picked one up and dropped it behind him with a small thud.

I cleared my throat. "Are you chaps, ah, not worried about another cave-in?" (I was quite proud of how steady my voice was. *I* certainly wasn't worried about a cave-in, it said, but *other* people might be.)

Ingold glanced up to see both Denton and me waiting expectantly. "What? Why are you looking at me?"

"You're the one who knows about coal mines," I said.

"I know about *coal*. It's different."

"But the firedamp and the poison water . . ."

Ingold's lips skewed sideways as he scowled. "That's *chemistry*. I like chemistry. Cave-ins and whatnot are . . ." He gazed up at the scarred rock of the ceiling. "*Architecture*."

I have heard military men scream obscenities under enemy fire with less venom. "I see. Not fond of architecture?"

"My aunt wanted me to be an architect."

I made a mental note to avoid meeting Ingold's aunt at all costs.

"Hopefully this all came down during blasting," Denton said. He picked up another rock and tossed it behind him.

"You can do that tomorrow," Ingold said firmly. "It's late and some of us have been down here for hours already."

I made another mental note to have Ingold canonized.

Denton sighed. "Tomorrow," he agreed, turning back. "We'll . . . ah . . . Easton, I can't help but notice you're going through that fellow's pockets."

"I'm part quartermaster," I said. Denton laughed. Ingold looked at us, baffled. I pulled a handful of bills from the trousers on the ground, all wadded up in the pocket, along with several loose coins.

"No wallet. No coin purse. But . . . oh, *here* we go . . ."

Wedged in among the bills was a receipt from the telegraph office.

"You're telling me this fellow sends a telegram pretending to be your cousin, comes back here, and changes clothes halfway down a mine," Angus said, after we had climbed back up the shaft. "On the other side of a cave-in."

"If you've got another explanation, I'm listening," Denton said.

"Perhaps it'll be clearer in the morning," Ingold said hopefully.

Angus's mustache expressed definite skepticism on this point, but he didn't argue. We went to bed, but it was a long time before I got the image of that strange, facedown pile of clothes out of my mind.

In the morning, not only was nothing clearer, it had gotten, if anything, murkier. I crawled out of my bedroll to find the others standing around one of the tables about ten feet inside the mine entrance, staring at a sheet of paper.

"Christ's blood, now what?" I asked. Kent appeared and pressed coffee into my hands. I blessed him and all his kin and swore undying fealty to his house. It took several sips of coffee before I realized I'd been speaking Gallacian, which was probably just as well.

"It appears that someone has left us a note," said Denton when I repeated myself in English.

The letter was oddly written. I don't mean the content, because I didn't focus on that for a few seconds, but the writing itself. It was written in ink, in a large, neat script, all the letters of the first line slanting to the right. And the next line was almost the exact same script, except that all the letters slanted to the left. It looked almost as if the writer had gotten to the end of the line, dropped down, changed direction, and begun writing from right to left instead. It reversed again at the next line, then stopped because it was quite a short note.

PLEASE GO AWAY AT ONCE. THE MINE IS UNSAFE FOR HUMANS AND YOU WILL BE IN GRAVE DANGER IF YOU CONTINUE TO STAY. THERE IS NOTHING OF VALUE FOR YOU HERE.

". . . Huh," I said. The word *humans* jumped out at me. I was pretty sure that wasn't the sort of word that you'd normally use there—you'd say *people* instead. In Gallacian, they'd be the same word, of course, but using the wrong one in English was the sort of mistake that pegged you as not a native speaker. Probably no one would correct you, or if they did, they'd be sure to say how well you spoke English, as if you were performing a trick. But it was still not quite the right word.

Ingold agreed with me. "But I don't think it's a threat," he added. "I suppose you could read it like one, but I don't think that was the intent."

"So what *was* the intent? Why scare us off?"

Kent cleared his throat. I was so used to him quietly arranging things in the background that it was startling to hear him speak up. "Perhaps someone wishes to reopen the mine?"

"It's failed twice as a coal mine," said Denton doubtfully.

"There are other things than coal, sir."

"That's true," said Ingold slowly. "If they found some valuable deposit, that might explain why they wish to keep people away."

"More importantly," said Denton, "*who* left it? Our friend from the telegraph office?"

"Maybe he came back for his clothes," I said. No one laughed.

"Whoever it was, they came in here where we were sleeping," Angus pointed out. "I'm not saying we wouldn't have woken up if they tried to get into one of the buildings, but I don't much like the thought of someone slinking around here at night."

"But did they come from town or up from the mine?" I asked, and then realized, by the quality of the silence, that everyone had been carefully not asking that question. I took a hasty gulp of coffee and burned the roof of my mouth.

"Either way is possible," Ingold said. "But they'd have to be awfully small to fit through that gap, assuming they were the one with the light."

"Go armed," Angus said. "A small man can kill you as dead as a big one."

Ingold grimaced. "A gunshot down there could bring the ceiling down."

"So maybe you'll take him with you."

There was no arguing with this logic. Denton holstered a gun and then he and Ingold went back down into the shaft to clear more rubble from the cave-in. I didn't volunteer to go along this time. Even I eventually run out of the need to prove myself to myself.

Instead I stayed up top and watched Angus and Kent watching each other. It's always a crapshoot with two extremely competent aide-de-camp types. Either they recognize a kindred spirit and begin sharing recipes for boot polish and how to feed fifty people on two turnips and an elderly onion, or they get along like a house fire, the kind with lots of screaming and hideous injuries.

Fortunately for domestic harmony, neither Angus nor Kent showed signs of incipient combustion. They divided the camp chores neatly between them and went to work. I went out and checked the horses, then came back and asked if I could help and was set to peeling potatoes. (Ironically, I did not actually peel many potatoes in the army. I was an officer. But prior to that, when I was a wide-eyed youngster in my mother's kitchen, I peeled my weight in potatoes weekly. This is not a skill you forget.)

It was, overall, an uneventful day. Denton and Ingold came up a few hours later, blinking in the daylight, and announced that they had cleared most of the rubble. "No sign of any red light," Denton said. "But there *is* a tunnel leading down. Though our mother hen here won't let me go into it just yet."

"Cluck cluck," said Ingold, unruffled. "You've got to give it a chance to air out. I want to build the fire up at the top of the ventilation shaft and see if we can't draw more air through."

So, after peeling potatoes, the rest of my day was spent gathering firewood. Honestly, it was like being back in Gallacia. It was even cold that night, and the bedroll felt like sheets of ice on my skin, which would have made me homesick if I had any desire to ever go home again.

I woke in the middle of the night because I had to piss like a racehorse. (Which is an odd phrase when you think of it. Do racehorses piss more than other horses? Why single them out for an analogy?) I made my way down the little steps of the overseer's shack and out past where we'd picketed the horses. The wooden latrine was of the board-with-a-hole variety, though Kent had cleared out the cobwebs and evicted any local spiders.

One thing that no one warns you about is how *loud* the nights are in America, or at least in West Virginia. There were the horses, of course, shifting their feet and making the occasional quiet snort, but that was almost drowned out by other *things*. Things that buzzed and chirped and croaked from every direction as I attended to matters. Were they all insects of some sort? Frogs? Birds? All three? The buzzing was probably an insect, but what was the thing that sounded like someone dragging their nail over a comb, or the one in the distance singing "Hwwih-poor-*will*! Hwwih-poor-*will*!" with monotonous enthusiasm?

There is nothing like having your trousers around your ankles and your arse hanging over an empty space while a veritable army of unseen nature screams at you to make you feel vulnerable. I finished with as much haste as I could and scurried back to the relative safety of the mine.

My foot had just hit the stairs to the overseer's office when I saw the red light coming from the mine shaft.

If it had not been so dark, I don't know that I would have seen it at all, but in the absolute blackness of the mine, it shone with a dull scarlet radiance. I froze, one hand still on my buttons, watching the red light shift across the stone ceiling. It didn't look like a lantern. This was a wriggling, moving light, slowly growing fainter as I watched.

I don't know what I was thinking. I wasn't armed and

had no lamp. Probably I should have woken the others at once. But all I could think of was laying eyes on what was causing it. I scurried across the floor to the entrance to the shaft and peered down.

Partway down, something glowed.

It was low to the ground, almost flat. At first I thought it was a person lying spread-eagled on a blanket. I could make out arms and legs, head and trunk, all shining a strange dull red. Recognizably human, even if it looked like it was made of melted candle wax.

Then it moved.

What I thought was a blanket was actually a thick ribbon of flesh that *crawled*, undulating with the too-fast ripple of a centipede's legs, as the thing went slithering across the ground, engulfed in bloody light.

I think if it had not had the human-shaped form atop it, I could have borne it better. It would have been shocking and unexpected, but my first thought would have been slugs or snails or flatworms. But the merging of alien movement with a half-melted human form was too much, and I stumbled back with a curse on my lips and my mind full of wailing horror.

Instantly the light went out. I stood frozen in the sudden darkness, terrified to move. Had the thing seen me? Had it heard me?

Was it already coming back this way?

If I moved, would it pinpoint my position and come rippling up the shaft to engulf me with no-longer-glowing flesh?

The mine's breath moaned out past me, bringing with it a scent of old buried things. It broke my paralysis and I bolted.

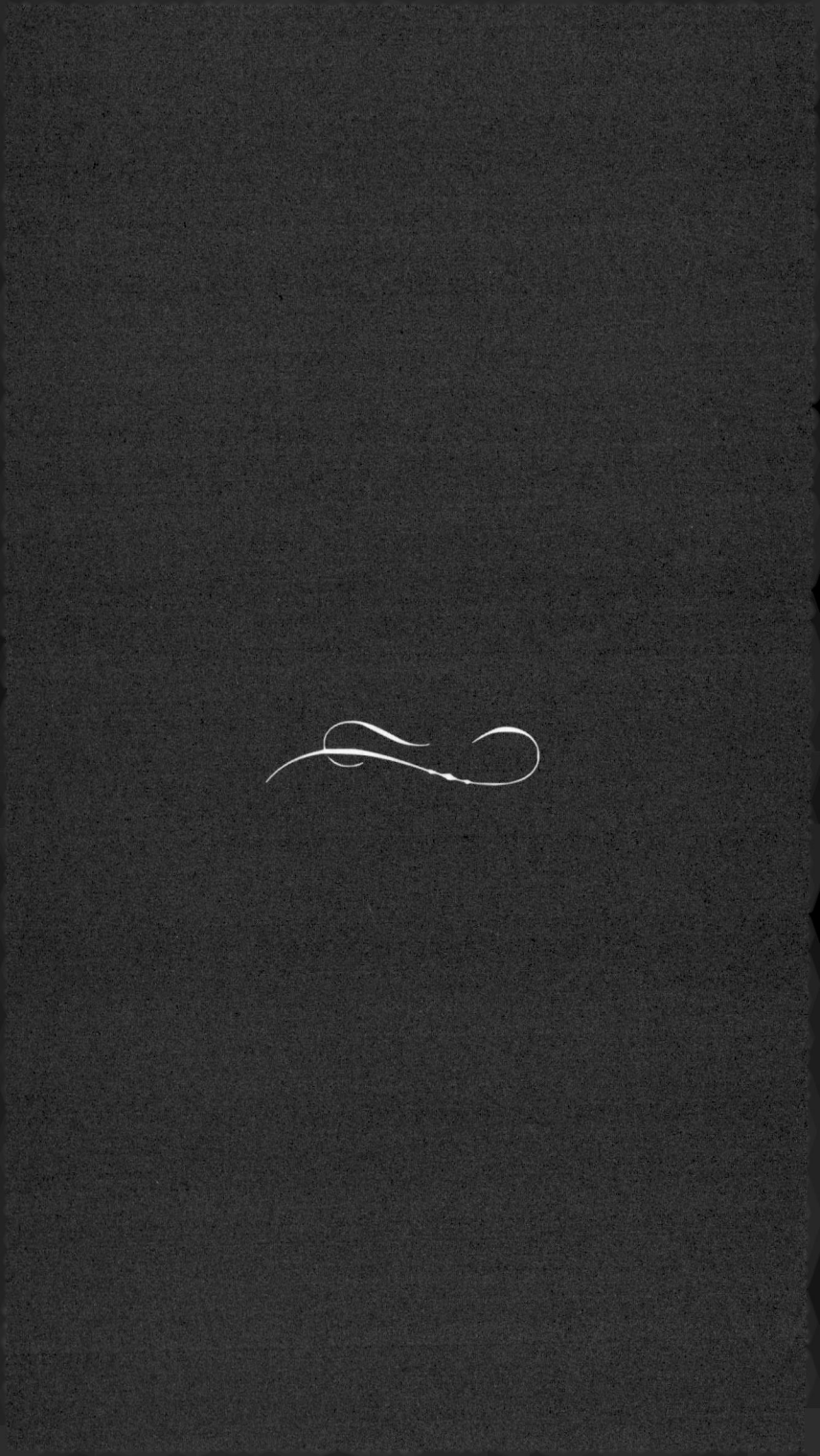

CHAPTER 8

"I know how it sounds," I said wearily. "Like a snail with a human body on top instead of a shell. But it was horrible."

"I believe you," said Ingold. "I just wish you'd woken me in time to see it."

I almost said, *No, you don't,* but thought better of it. Ingold *would* have wanted to see it. He would probably have found it fascinating. He was that sort of person.

"Do you think it was what was following you two earlier?" Denton asked.

"It almost has to be, doesn't it?" I thought of the way the flat thing had moved. Yes, it would probably make wet slapping sounds like that. "What are the odds of *two* horrible inhuman things lurking in the mine?"

"What are the odds of *one* horrible inhuman thing lurking in the mine?" Angus said dryly.

"We don't know that it's horrible," Ingold pointed out.

"It didn't do anything to us, and presumably it would have had the opportunity."

"It did something to Oscar," said Denton.

"We don't know *that* either," Ingold said, with more truth than tact. "Unless you think it's in league with the man from the telegraph office."

It was hard to imagine any human being in league with the thing I'd seen. You might as well be in league with a snail or an octopus.

We sat around the fire, which Kent had rekindled from embers. It was so late it had become early, and I was busy second-guessing what I had seen. Maybe I hadn't gotten that good a look at it. Maybe I'd seen a person on all fours and my brain had made up the details, aided by the low light and probably some of Ingold's firedamp fumes.

A few years ago, I'd have said that my brain couldn't have come up with anything quite so bizarre, but I had lived through some things since then. Still, this seemed a little bit beyond the limits of my imagination. Big things with teeth, certainly. Any horrible thing involving mushrooms, sadly. But a flattened-out human slug-thing? Even for me, that was a bit much. Despite what you might think, I'm not a particularly fanciful person.

And there remained the fact that I had heard the wet slapping sound, and then Ingold and Denton had heard it, too.

No matter how I tried to turn it around in my head, I was pretty sure I'd seen something awful and inexplicable in the mine shaft. Something that had been *right there*, only a dozen yards from the top, something that could have been *up here*. Something that could have been hiding in the darkness, underneath one of the dozens of ruined bits of machinery, watching us. You might walk by it a dozen times and never think anything of it, because that space was much too small for a human being to fit.

The mine is unsafe for humans . . .

Christ's blood, maybe that hadn't been the wrong choice of words after all.

I opened my mouth to say something of the sort, when Angus's head jerked to one side and he held up a hand.

"There's something out there," he said, gazing outside the mine entrance.

"Dangerous?" asked Ingold.

"Big," said Angus, which didn't quite answer the question. I reached casually for my pistol.

A moment later we heard scrambling footsteps and saw a light approaching. *Human,* I thought, and relaxed, though only slightly. (I've known too many humans.)

"Hello?" our visitor called. "Doctor? Are you there?"

Denton opened his mouth, but Angus beat him to it. "Who's asking?"

Firelight shone on a tall figure, wearing a familiar hat. It was Stovepipe from the camp, looking both bedraggled and slightly frantic. "Me, Elijah," he said. He scanned the circle of faces, settled on Denton's. "Roger said you were a doctor. Will you come? There's been an attack. Lousia's hurt bad."

"How bad?" Denton was already scrambling to his feet.

"Bear got her," said Elijah. "Got Lee Mason first. She near tripped over them both. Tore her arm all to pieces. She needs help."

"Yes, of course. Just let me grab my bag. Ingold, will you come?"

"Of course."

Angus and I exchanged a single speaking look. The odds were good that Elijah was telling the truth, but if he wasn't, Ingold and Denton could be walking into a trap. And while they might be able to defend themselves, Denton was a surgeon, not a soldier. On the other hand, neither of us wanted to leave Kent alone or the campsite unguarded. I suspected that Kent could defend himself quite well with a frying pan, if it came to that, but one person is a helluva lot more vulnerable than two.

"I'll come with you," I told Denton, "if there's a bear about. Are we taking the horses?"

Elijah shook his head. "Too dark. Faster as the crow flies," he said, gesturing to the wooded slope behind him. "But we gotta hurry."

"I'm ready," said Denton, and the three of us followed the man and his stovepipe hat out into the night.

It was indeed faster as the crow flies. We were only about two miles from the shantytown, but it wasn't an easy walk. Leftover rock extracted from the mine made an ankle-breaking slope coated in wet leaves from the nearby trees, and a couple of times I thought that Denton was going to be treating one of us before we ever got there. But then the ground evened out and turned into scrubby woodland, overgrown with briars and thorny vines. I concentrated on following exactly in Elijah's footsteps, and before long we were coming around into the camp from the opposite direction as last time.

"Keep your eyes peeled," Elijah said. "Bear's still out there."

I put my hand on the butt of my pistol, while thinking that "keep your eyes peeled" was a horrifying turn of phrase. I generally quite like English, don't get me wrong—it lacks a great many pronouns, but it has so many other words to cover every shade of meaning. But Christ's blood, what an image. I imagined someone scraping my eyeballs with a knife, peeling the corneas off the way I'd peeled potatoes for Kent last night.

We did not see a bear. I can't say I was disappointed. Pistols are not what you want to have in hand if a bear is charging at you. I would prefer a rifle to a pistol and a ticket to another country to either. I hear that Guam is lovely this time of year.

Elijah took us to a shack that was larger and cleaner than Roger's had been. A dog barked at us until he shushed it and opened the door. A woman lay on the bed inside, her arm wrapped in a blood-soaked wad of clothing. Denton stepped in, all business, and pulled the makeshift bandage back, whereupon I found a pressing reason to be outside. (I don't mind injuries on dead bodies, but the same injury on a *living* person can turn my stomach. I got far too much of that during the war.)

I sat down on the step. The dog whined at me, a brownish mutt that was mostly hound, judging by the ears. It flattened itself and approached hopefully, and I held out my fingers.

Unlike Thunder, this dog was delighted to sniff me, and then to try to convince me that it had never been petted in its life. I rubbed its ears, and it leaned against my legs and sighed. "Rough night for you too, huh?" I asked. "Your humans running around and yelling and getting hurt." The dog sighed again, more deeply.

The door opened and Ingold joined me outside. I couldn't imagine that he was squeamish the same way I was—doubtless he'd find grievous wounds just so *interesting*—so I wasn't surprised when he said, "Elijah said the dead body is behind the building."

I've seen enough dead bodies for a hundred lifetimes and didn't really feel the need to examine this one, but I also didn't want to let Ingold wander around and possibly be eaten by a bear. I reluctantly pushed the dog off my legs and followed him around the back of the shack, where there was, indeed, a suspiciously body-shaped lump underneath a blanket. I gazed off into the dark, looking for bears. A Gallacian bear would be long gone after having been scared off, but might return a day or two later if it thought there was food. Were American bears similar? Did they try to shake hands with you before they attacked?

Ingold crouched down and lifted the blanket, then let out a low whistle. "Easton? Come take a look at this, will you?"

I stifled a sigh and padded over. Ingold folded back the blanket and moved the lantern to get a better view.

It took me a moment to make sense of what I was seeing. The body was of an older man. What was left of it, anyway. The abdomen was simply *gone*, flesh and organs torn away until I could see the exposed backbone. Not the worst corpse I've ever seen, but certainly not a pleasant sight.

"Have you ever seen an animal attack that looked like this?" Ingold asked quietly, tilting the lantern until he could see into the rib cage. It was practically hollow inside, absent lungs or heart or anything else.

"No," I said. "But I don't know anything about American bear attacks."

"Well, I do," said Ingold, "and they don't look like this."

"It looks almost like . . ." I stopped, hardly wanting to finish the thought. "It looks like somebody gutted him like a deer," I finally said.

"Exactly. Most predators will go for the viscera, of course, but they don't clean their prey out like this." He sat back, frowning.

"You think a person did this?" I asked, keeping my voice low so that they couldn't hear me inside the house.

Ingold dropped the blanket back over the dead man's face. "I think that very few bears unbutton somebody's trousers so they can get a better shot at his guts."

Christ's blood. "You think . . . ah . . . it could be the thing from the mine?" I really didn't want to think of it getting up and leaving the mine. If there was a horrible thing in the earth, it should *stay* in the earth, not get up and wander around the countryside. Particularly not when I had to walk two miles through that countryside in the dark.

Ingold shrugged helplessly. "The thought had occurred to me, but how could we tell? We don't have enough information. And for all I know, this poor fellow was taking a piss when the . . . the whatever-it-was got him."

He rose to his feet. "We are drowning in ignorance at the moment. And the only place with possible answers seems to be deeper in the mine."

I turned away from the body. "I was afraid you were going to say that."

Denton emerged from the shed an hour later, bloody but quietly satisfied. "It'll be touch and go with infection, but the wound itself won't kill her."

"Did she say it was a bear that she saw?" asked Ingold.

"With the amount of whiskey they poured down her, I doubt she'd remember seeing the president," said Denton. "Anyway, there's nothing more that I can do for her now. I'll check back on her tomorrow." He rubbed his face, leaving a smear of blood that shone black in the lantern light.

"Come look at this," Ingold said, beckoning him over to the corpse. I had no desire to look at it again, but a thought had occurred to me. I could see Roger's shack only a few dozen yards away, a black outline on the gray-black of the hillside.

I excused myself from the dog again and made my way over to it. He probably hadn't seen anything—was probably drunk right now, as a matter of fact—but I could ask.

Well, I could have asked if he answered the door, but he didn't. Even hammering on it didn't wake him, assuming that he was inside at all. I listened, trying to make out snoring, but couldn't hear anything over the cacophony of America's nighttime wildlife.

I thought about opening the door and stepping inside, but breaking into the house of a drunken man with a gun and a guard dog seemed like an excellent way to get shot, so I abandoned the thought and went to rejoin Ingold and Denton.

It was only as I was slipping and slithering my way across the rubble back to the mine that it occurred to me that Roger's dog hadn't barked at me either.

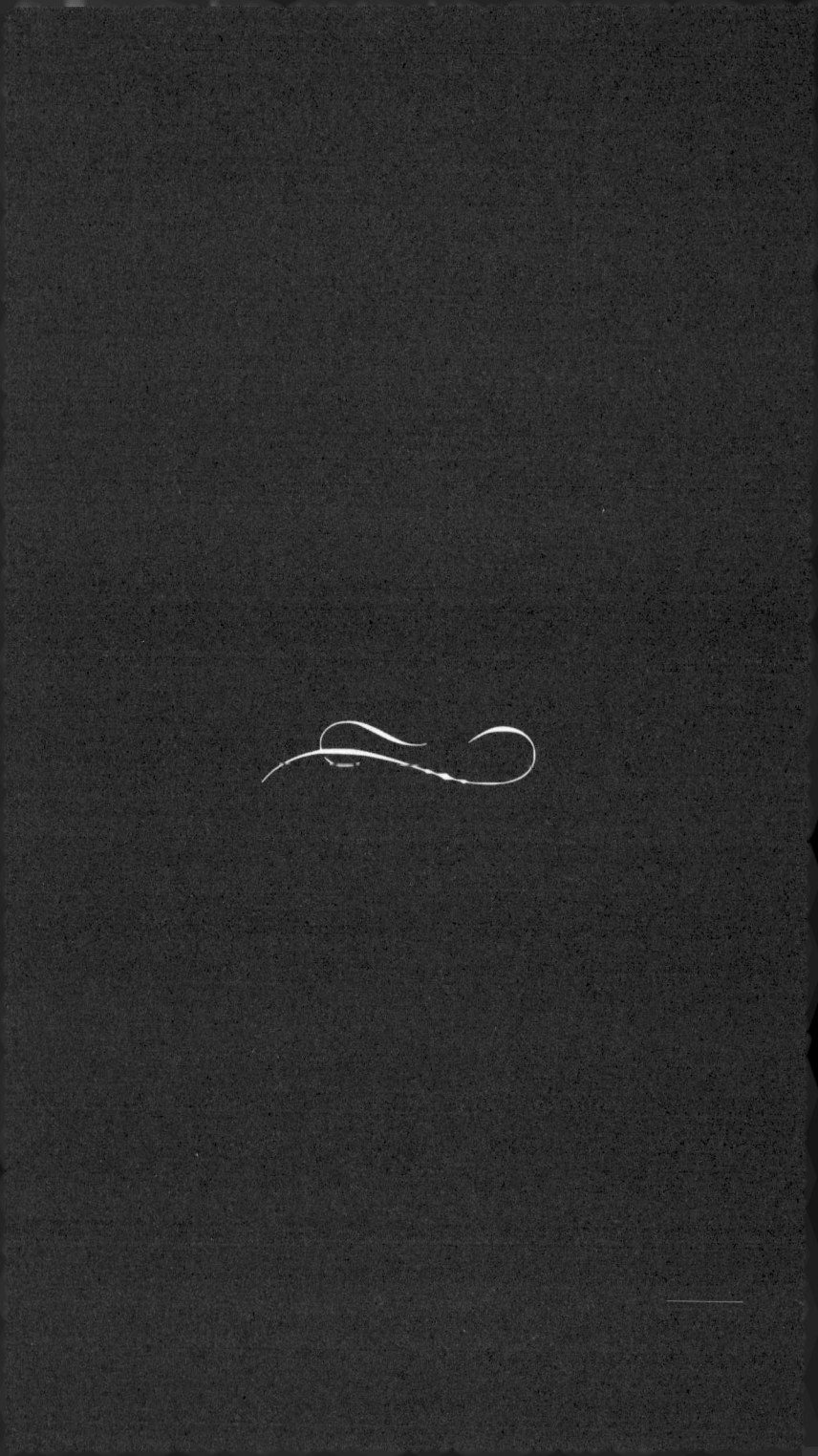

CHAPTER 9

After our adventures of the night before, I slept late. By the time I woke up, Denton was already down in the mine, clearing rubble like a man obsessed.

Kent delivered this information to me, then poured the coffee with his lips pressed tightly together. Even someone as oblivious as I am could detect the signs that Kent was worried about his employer.

"He's working himself awfully hard," I offered, tossing the words out like bait.

"Too hard," said Kent savagely. "It isn't healthy. And he's not as young as he used to be." He stopped there, sniffed, and said, in a slightly more controlled voice, "Of course, he is a doctor, and I'm sure he knows what he's about."

"Oh, certainly. Though I'm told that doctors often make the worst patients."

Kent exhaled through his nostrils in a sound that was

just this side of a snort. "Indeed," he said, and retired to the other side of our camp to wash dishes.

If Kent was willing to break the code of the gentleman's gentleman enough to express concern, Denton must be acting more erratically than I realized. But then again, what did I know? I'd only seen him under dire circumstances, after all.

I sat on a rock outside the mine entrance, soaking up the sun. The cacophony of night creatures had been replaced by the ripple of wind through the trees. Each ripple sent leaves spinning down to the ground. It was cool, despite the sun.

It was going to be a lot cooler underground. I picked up my headlamp, collected Angus, and strolled down into the mine.

"Alex!" Denton looked up at me with apparent delight. "We've just now opened the way through. You're just in time."

"Excellent," I lied.

Denton was the first one through the new-made gap in the rockfall. Ingold gestured at me to go next, and I scrambled through. It was a much longer crawl than I'd expected, a good dozen feet through loose rubble. My knees cursed me with every step.

On the far side, Denton was practically dancing with impatience. As soon as Angus was through, he set off into the dark.

The tunnel turned sharply to the left, still sloping downward, and we followed, while I listened desperately for sounds of the glowing thing I'd seen before. I heard nothing but our own footsteps. *Perhaps it didn't come this way at all*, I thought hopefully, and then we turned the corner and confronted a wall.

The beam of Denton's headlamp swung from side to side as he looked for a way past. I stepped back, torn between disappointment and relief that maybe we could leave this place before encountering another cave-in.

But it was not to be. Denton crowed with triumph and rushed forward to a dark hole at the base of the wall. "Down here," he said. "There's a way down."

I took a step forward and my boot hit something that went *clink* instead of *thunk*. It was an empty tin can. I turned it over and saw the remains of a shredded label for stew pasted to the side.

"Like Oscar described in his letter," Denton said excitedly. "This *must* be the place he was talking about. Which means that the chamber should be at the bottom of this tunnel."

Ingold leaned over the tunnel and looked down. His expression was well past dubious and picking up speed. ". . . Um," he said.

Denton was already on his hands and knees, his head vanishing inside. I joined Ingold at the edge of the hole and my stomach did not so much clench as reach up and grab my esophagus while screaming obscenities. If someone had designed my own personal hell, the entryway would probably look like that.

It was less a tunnel than a crawl space, going downward in a tight curve, like a spiral staircase designed for badgers. Anyone entering would have to go on their hands and knees, with no way to turn around unless the crawl space opened up somewhere out of sight.

"Denton—" Ingold began.

The doctor was already crawling inside. "It keeps going," he called back. "I'll just—"

"*Denton.*"

Ingold's voice cracked like a whip. Denton jerked in surprise and his helmet knocked against the ceiling. He backed out of the crawl space and sat back on his heels. "What's wrong?"

"Listen to me," said Ingold. "If you go down, you're going alone. We can't—*I* can't—That crawl space is a *death trap*." He reached out a hand as if to catch Denton's, then pulled it back. "If you hit a pocket of gas, even if someone went with you, they couldn't pull you back out before it got to them, too. Which means if something happens to you, we won't be able to rescue you."

"I understand," Denton said. "It's fine. I know the risks."

"Do you?" Had Ingold gone pale under the smears of soot, or was that an artifact of the light? "Denton, if you break a leg or somehow get trapped under rubble, you'll *die* down there. Of shock if you're lucky. Thirst if you're not. Are you really sure you want to do this?"

"If Oscar came this way, then there's a way through," he said stubbornly.

"Denton . . ." I reached out and gripped his shoulder. Probably it was a time for tact, but that's never been a skill of mine. I settled for bald honesty. "Denton, Oscar *has* to be dead by now. You don't have to do this."

He shook his head. "Yes, I do. He saved my life when I was seven. I broke through the ice on the lake behind the house and went under. He went under the ice after me, even though he could have died, too. I owe it to him to try."

Ingold's throat worked, and then he simply said, "I don't want you to go."

"I know." Denton bowed his head, and I remembered that he and I had seen the dead get up and walk two years ago. I don't know if he was thinking that Oscar might still be down there, dead but still moving. Maybe he had to know for sure.

"Fine," said Ingold wearily, when the moment had stretched out past all bearing. "Do what you have to do. If you're not back in a few hours, we'll assume you're dead."

"Fair," said Denton, and began crawling back down into the twisting hole in the floor. I watched until the light had vanished and prayed to the God I only half believed in that I'd see the doctor again.

It was a nightmarish wait. We could have just gone back up, I suppose, but leaving felt like consigning Denton to the ranks of the dead. Ingold kept pulling out his pocket watch and staring at it, then putting it back, only to pull it out again a minute later, as if he'd already forgotten what it said. Angus disassembled his pistol and began carefully cleaning each part.

The mine sighed and whispered around us. I sat against the wall, watching back the way we had come for any sign of red light. Though the creature seemed to be able to turn it off at will, so perhaps I wouldn't see it coming. Maybe it would just appear, rushing out of the dark, a wave of flesh that would crash over us and . . .

My imagination failed at that point, but I was certain it wouldn't be anything good.

"Hey, Angus?"

"Aye?"

"If you thought my body was at the bottom of a mine shaft, would you crawl down to get it?"

"Are you serious?" asked my dearest friend. "I'd throw a bottle of livrit down after you, toast your memory, and be on the next boat back to Gallacia." He considered for a moment, then added, "I might find a convent and ask them to pray for your soul. That's as far as I go."

"Oh, thank God." I closed my eyes. The idea of anyone putting themselves in danger to retrieve my body was horrifying. Maybe that was the difference between me and Denton. Surgeons see the bodies that get brought back, so maybe they don't all learn to give up on the ones that are never coming back.

"He was very scarred by what you faced in Ruravia," Ingold said abruptly.

I looked up, startled. "We all were," I said finally. "It was . . . not a good thing to experience."

"It brought many memories back for him, of the war."

I nodded. Angus grunted.

The war had receded for me in recent months, thanks mostly to time and a very wise young man named Bors, but I understood. The immediate aftermath of our experience with Usher's lake had left me sleepless and afraid. I wasn't surprised that it had taken Denton the same way.

"Now he's convinced that what's happening *here* is akin to what happened *there*, and it's driving him recklessly." Ingold stared down into the hole in the floor and added, half under his breath, "I should not have let him go."

"You'd have had a hard time stopping him," Angus said, beginning to reassemble his gun. "Unless you wanted us to hold him down and sit on him."

I suspected that Ingold would have been happier if we'd tried, but before he could say anything, we heard the scuffle of something ascending the crawlspace from below.

The light that emerged was the actinic white of a headlamp, not the bloody red of . . . whatever the hell it was . . . which is the only reason that I didn't turn tail and run like a rabbit. A moment later, Denton's head popped up out of the hole, and he looked at us all with a broad grin. "It's a long crawl down, sort of spiral shaped, but it opens up at the bottom. And you won't *believe* what's down there."

Crawling down the spiral shaft was worse than I had imagined. My shoulder pressed against the outer wall and my helmet kept scraping against the ceiling. Even though Denton said that it opened up below, I was having a hard time believing it. It seemed more likely that it would just keep going, narrowing farther, until I had to choose between going forward or going back. And Angus was behind me, so I couldn't go back. He'd have to back all the way out, and then I would, and what if he got stuck like a cork in a wine bottle and then I would have no way out and we would both be trapped and we'd die in here and no one would ever find our bodies.

The walls began to undulate strangely. At first I thought that I was getting dizzy, but no, the outer wall actually swept in and then back out every few feet, so keeping my shoulder to the wall made me feel like I was wobbling downward. The alternative was to abandon the wall, though, and that didn't bear thinking about.

I kept going. The stone had bands of color, long horizontal bands. Strata, I think Ingold had called them. We were climbing down through strata. I could see Denton's heels as he crawled down in front of me. Why was he going so slowly? He'd been down here once already, he said that it was safe, but I was practically on top of him now and how much air was there in the shaft, really? Was it getting stale or was I panicking?

Blessed Virgin, I prayed, *if I'm going to die down here, let my last view not be Denton's arse.*

I closed my eyes. That meant that I couldn't see how narrow the space was. I just had to keep my shoulder against the left wall. If I didn't touch the right one, I wouldn't have to know how close it was. I kept crawling, around and around, boring into the earth. Who had made a tunnel like this? It couldn't be natural. The floor felt smooth, almost polished. Christ's blood, why couldn't they have just made a hole straight down and run a ladder instead?

It occurred to me that if you were a low, fleshy horizontal thing that glowed redly in the dark, maybe this was just the sort of tunnel you'd make. It had fled from us before, and this winding hole seemed like the only place it could have disappeared into. Maybe it was waiting at the bottom, or maybe it was even now creeping in after us and soon we would hear the wet echoes of its passage trapping us in from behind . . .

My foot banged into the right-hand wall and it was so close, closer than I'd thought. I couldn't get enough air.

Had I stopped moving? No, Angus would have thumped me. I must still be moving. I could hear the harsh echoes of my breathing in a space that I didn't dare look at again.

When the wall fell away from my left shoulder, I almost didn't notice. I kept crawling forward, eyes squeezed shut, even though the ground was no longer sloping, even though the echoes were suddenly different and part of me knew that I was in a much larger space but the rest of me was still crawling downward and would be forever, world without end, amen.

Denton said, "Easton?" and my eyes snapped open.

I was out. I was through. The walls were far away. I had nearly run into Denton, who was standing. I stood up too, feeling my hips and back scream at me, but I barely noticed. Our hellish descent was almost forgotten.

We stood inside a chamber made of pearl and glory.

The floor of the chamber was slick and shiny, a highly polished sheet of . . . something. It shimmered with iridescent rainbows, like a vast sheet of pearl. Either the floor was translucent and there was light somewhere under it, or it glowed very faintly in the dark.

Have you ever seen an abalone shell? They're not terribly common in Europe, I don't think. I've mostly seen them used as jewelry. This surface reminded me of those shells, only softer, more pinks and purples than blues and greens. The walls were white limestone, hung with stalag . . . stalac . . . the ones that hang down, okay? The pale glow of the floor reflected off the bottom few inches of the white walls, giving the farthest reaches of the cave a hazy look.

"Good lord," said Denton softly.

"It's beautiful," said Ingold, lifting his lantern.

I put my hand to the floor, half expecting it to feel warm, but it felt like cold glass. Perhaps there was some kind of clear glaze over the surface. Even in the lamplight, I could see my hand reflecting faintly in the glaze. The pearlescent surface edged the shadow with rainbow reflections.

"Can you imagine what people would pay for this stuff?" asked Denton. "To use in place of marble?"

"Spoken like a true industrialist," said Ingold dryly.

"Someone's tried," Angus said, pointing. Off to one side, a rusted hand drill lay discarded on the floor. I ambled over, knelt down, and ran my hand over the floor. I couldn't see anything, but my fingertips picked up the tiniest scuff mark on the surface. I wondered how long it had taken to drill that much. I sat back, watching the others survey the chamber. Ingold was peering closely at the floor. Denton was walking back and forth, as if trying to take in all that he was seeing. Angus completed a circuit of the perimeter and returned. "No other way in, unless you're a bat," he said, to no one in particular. I nodded anyway. I could see a few dark cracks in the stone roof. *That must be the cause of the mine breathing,* I thought, and then felt rather smug that I'd internalized that much of Ingold's lectures on caverns.

The glassy surface, though beautiful, was punishingly hard on my knees. I met my own reflection's gaze and snorted. I looked like hell.

I turned my head to speak to Angus and my reflection turned the other direction.

What I was seeing in my peripheral vision was so impossible that for a moment I didn't recognize what had happened. My eyes reported that something was wrong and I jerked my head back, expecting to see something terrible and concrete—the reflection of a monster bearing down on me, perhaps, or a crack in the floor that threatened to tumble me down into the depths of the mine.

Only my own face looked back, pearly with rainbows. But when I turned my head to the right, it shifted left. A reversed image, but not a mirrored one.

Dread slid cool fingers up my spine.

I turned my head again, very slowly, and the reflection mimicked me in reverse. Its expression was a perfect match for my own, assuming that I was currently slack-jawed, which I'm pretty sure I was.

I slid my hand upward along the floor and my reflection's hand moved with it. I jerked it free suddenly, and for an instant, I looked down on my reflection's palm pressed against the glass before it caught up.

"Angus," I said. I sounded remarkably calm. "Angus, please come and tell me that you see what I see."

Angus stomped over and looked over my shoulder. "What? I don't see . . ."

He trailed off. I moved back and forth and the reflection moved with me, as if I had an identical twin beneath the surface of the floor.

Angus went down on his knees next to me, and I saw his face join mine. When we looked at each other, our reflections gazed off to the corners of the room. When we looked over our shoulders, our reflections locked eyes with each other.

"What *is* it?" he said softly.

"Damned if I know." I sat back on my heels.

Our reflections didn't vanish. They stayed where they had been, gazing up at us. As I watched, my face opened its mouth, revealing rows of pearl teeth, in a silent scream of horror.

CHAPTER 10

I snapped my mouth shut as soon as I realized what was happening. So did my reflection. Yes, I was horrified. I could admit that. I just didn't want anyone else to see it. The sweat that had sprung up in that terrible downward crawl was freezing on my body, and it wasn't just the cold of the room.

"Ingold," I said, very carefully. "Denton. There's something going on here that you should see."

They must have heard something in my voice because they came over at once. "Look at the reflections," I said, turning my head.

Ingold let out a low whistle. Denton actually jumped, like a cat catching sight of a snake, his feet skidding on the slick floor. "What the *hell* . . . ?"

Ingold brought the lantern as close to the surface as he could. The fire gleamed strangely between our mirrored faces, and then suddenly color spasmed across the pearlescent surface, great gouts of red and white and orange, as if in imitation of the flame. I stood up. I wasn't sure if an extra foot or two of height would help at all, but I didn't like the way the colors spread. They bloomed out in circles, like ink soaking through paper. Our faces were filled with rings of bruising light.

Abruptly Ingold laughed. "Chromatophores!" he said, as the colors splattered across the floor. He sounded utterly delighted. I wished I had a tenth of his enthusiasm.

"Whatafores?"

"Darwin described them in cuttlefish. These... creatures... whatever they are, must possess something similar."

"Creatures?" I said.

"The floor is alive?" Denton said.

"You're saying the floor is made of *cuttlefish*?!" said Angus.

"No, no." Ingold laughed again, still staring at the fireworks display across the floor. "Many animals can change color. Chameleons, frogs, fish. It is hardly limited to one order of life. That may explain the mimicry as well. Most color-changing creatures do so to hide from predators, so possibly..." He trailed off. I fixated on the one bit that I understood.

"You're saying this *isn't* stone?" I asked, trying to back away from the floor, which went about as well as you'd expect.

"No," said Ingold. "Shell, probably. Some kind of protective surface over the creatures. Or creature. I suppose it could be only one."

The colors shifted, turning darker, browns and purples

replacing the brighter colors. It was still beautiful, but the sense of something *other* filled the room to choking, thick as firedamp. They felt wrong. It's hard to explain—how can a *color* be wrong?—but if I were pouring out ink or paint to make patterns, I would have chosen them differently and arranged them differently. These colors bled together in ways that I couldn't predict and wouldn't have expected. They felt *alien*. If I stared at them too long, I started to feel dizzy, as if I was looking down from an unexpectedly high place.

"If it's a shell," said Angus, ever the practical one, "are you saying this thing is some kind of shellfish? Like a giant oyster?"

"Maybe?" Ingold looked up, his eyes shining. Apparently the alienness affected him less than the rest of us. "But Denton, do you know what this means?"

Judging by Denton's expression, nothing good. His previous wonder had been wiped away by the sight of the moving faces below. (I could hardly blame him. So had mine.)

"It means Oscar wasn't hallucinating!" Ingold beamed at us, as if this was a joy and a delight instead of confirmation of all of Denton's worst fears.

"Good to know," said Angus. I was already backing toward the entryway. I hated that crawl space like I had hated few other things on earth, but standing on . . . whatever this was . . . made me queasy with dread. What if the hard surface was only there because the faces wanted it there? What if they could just open the floor like a mouth and swallow us all whole?

"I think I ... err ... forgot something ... at camp ..." I said, and bolted for the tunnel.

I was bathed in sweat by the time I got to the top of the rippling crawl. It was slightly less awful on the way up, but only because I knew that it didn't get any tighter. Didn't *squeeze*.

I rolled out of the opening to one side, knocked my headlamp against the wall, and sent it askew. I had to take it off to adjust it, which is why I was able to see the red light at the end of the corridor a moment later.

"Christ's blood," I muttered. My first thought was that it was just one damn thing after another. My second, much more important thought, was that I was alone up here with it.

I shoved my head down into the crawl space and yelled, "*The light's here!*" as loud as I could. I expected it to echo, but it didn't, probably because Angus was just coming out of the hole.

"Where, now?"

I pointed. Of course it had gone out by now. Angus pulled himself out, followed by Denton and a grumbling Ingold. "I don't know why we couldn't stay," he was saying. "Obviously there was something between us and the creatures—"

"Red light," I said, which stopped him immediately.

Denton took off down the tunnel. I went after him, nearly losing him at the squeeze, but we caught up again at the split in the tunnel. He was looking both ways, clearly frustrated.

"Two and two," Angus said, jerking his head toward me. "You take Denton left. Ingold and I will go right."

Denton bolted the moment he heard the word *left*. I ran after him, the beam of light bouncing crazily on his back. I couldn't remember what this branch was like. A dead end, I was pretty sure, though I wasn't sure how many twists it took to get there. "Denton, wait!"

It is somewhat embarrassing to be outpaced by a man half again your age. I told myself I was still recovering from the crawl. I managed to catch up to him and grab for his shoulder. The pain in my side felt like a bayonet.

"Denton . . . wait for . . ."

He shook me off. "There's a man down here! I'd nearly caught him!" And then he was off again, and I had to stop and put my hands on my knees and breathe until the spots in my vision went away.

Not ten seconds later, I heard a cry from the tunnel ahead. It was anguish and surprise all at once, and I would have thought that Denton had fallen into a hole and broken everything, except that what I heard was a single word, in Denton's voice.

"Oscar?!"

I skidded around the last turn in the corridor, gasping like a broken-winded horse. My light illuminated a tableau like the one of the posters plastered all over Paris advertising lurid plays—Denton against the far wall, caught in the beam, one hand outstretched; a second man, on his knees at the base of the wall, head thrown back. He wore an unlit headlamp and a thick set of mining goggles, giving him the look of some strange insect dug up in the far reaches of the earth.

Denton grabbed his shoulders, hauling him upright. "Oscar, it's me! Denton!"

The man's mouth opened and he took a step forward, lips silently forming Denton's name. That was all it took for the doctor to fling his arms around his cousin and begin pounding his back. "Oscar, I thought you were dead!"

When they finally separated, Denton was frowning. "What's wrong?"

Oscar smiled sheepishly and touched his throat, then shook his head. He reached into his pack and pulled out a green slate and a piece of chalk and wrote: SORRY. CAN'T TALK.

"You can't talk?"

He erased the slate with his sleeve. MINE GAS. HURT THROAT. DR SAID NOT TO.

"Good lord," said Denton. "You'll have to tell me all about it. Ah—sorry, here, let me introduce my friend. This is Lieutenant Easton."

"Why'd you run?" I managed to get out, without sounding too wheezy.

THOUGHT YOU WERE OTHER MEN.

"It's just us," Denton said. He laughed, brief and hysterical. "Have you been avoiding us all this time?"

Oscar tapped the slate over the words OTHER MEN and shrugged, with another sheepish smile.

"What other men?" I asked.

DON'T KNOW. CHASED UNTIL I GOT LOST.

Approaching footsteps heralded the arrival of Angus and Ingold. "We heard the yell," Ingold said. *He* didn't sound winded. He looked uncertainly from Oscar to Denton, then back again.

"I'm fine," said Denton. He laughed again, another half-hysterical bark. "Better than fine! This is Dr. John Ingold and Angus. Everyone, my cousin Oscar, who has given us quite a scare."

Oscar ducked his head, clearly embarrassed, and stood clutching the slate.

"We've been hunting all over for you," said Denton, after an awkward moment of silence. "And you've been here in the mine the whole time? Why didn't you answer any of my letters?"

Oscar shook his head. LOST, he wrote on the slate.

I was facing Oscar and Denton, my head turned a little to one side so as not to blind them with my lamp. That was probably why I saw Angus calmly reach down, lift his pistol, and point it at Denton's cousin.

The sound of the gun being cocked was extraordinarily loud in the tunnel.

"Angus, what are you—" Denton started.

"Take off your goggles," ordered Angus.

The man gazed at us in silence, his mouth a little open, as if he had been panting. Denton began to protest, but Angus lifted the gun half an inch. "*Do it*," he ordered.

Slowly, grudgingly, Denton's cousin lowered his head, covering his face with his hands, and pulled the goggles down. When he lifted his head again, his eyes were tightly closed.

"It's the light," said Denton angrily. "If he spent a long time in the cave, his eyes desensitized. The light hurts him."

"Open your eyes," grated Angus.

"Easton." Denton appealed to me, caught somewhere between exasperation and panic. "Easton, do something!"

"Angus is the wisest man I know," I said, which was true, even if I had no idea what he was getting at.

"But . . ." Denton's face held the peculiar expression of a man who knew that something was too good to be true, but maybe if he argued, he could keep it for just a little longer. "We can't . . ."

"Open. Your. Eyes."

Oscar held very still for a moment, and then his eyelids lifted. If I had not been watching so closely, I would not have thought he had opened them at all.

The eyes beneath had neither whites nor iris. They were the same color as his skin, the exact same shade of tan. For an instant I was reminded of Grecian statues, of white marble faces with blank white marble eyes.

Ingold swore in a language I didn't know.

Color bloomed suddenly across Oscar's face. White first, a splash across each eye socket, bleeding onto the lower lids and cheeks. Then a smaller blob of darkness in each one, the size of a thumbprint, darkening half the eye and the side of the nose.

White blobs with dark centers. A child's drawing of eyes, splashed across the face in a last desperate attempt to look human. My breath hissed through my teeth.

"Chromatophores," said Ingold quietly. "It can't make them quite small enough."

The thing that wasn't Oscar nodded at Ingold.

SHAPE EASY, the creature wrote on the slate. COLOR HARD.

"What *are* you?" hissed Denton.

The creature wiped the slate clean with his sleeve and wrote WE MEAN NO HARM.

"Do I shoot him?" asked Angus.

Not-Oscar stood completely still, holding the slate with his message. He must have understood what Angus said, but he made no effort to plead for his life.

I wondered if bullets could actually hurt him, and then immediately regretted wondering.

"Where is the real Oscar? Where is my cousin? *What have you done with him?*"

Ingold grabbed Denton before anyone could find out how his abortive lunge would end. The creature began shaking his head and hastily wrote WE DID NOTHING. He displayed the slate to Denton, still shaking his head, then wiped it clean and added, HE RAN AWAY.

"Can't blame him," muttered Angus.

"Ran away where?" asked Ingold, not letting go of his grip on Denton.

INTO TUNNELS. WE COULD NOT FIND HIM.

"Why were you looking for him?" Denton asked, his voice high and sharp.

The creature's expression did not change, but it hesitated before writing, as if confused by the question. TUNNELS ARE DANGEROUS.

"You expect me to believe that he ran off and you chased him out of the goodness of your heart?"

Not-Oscar began shaking his head again. WE MEAN NO HARM. ONLY TALK.

I figured that it was my turn to speak up. "So why pretend to *be* Oscar?"

Those strange, wrong-colored eyes turned toward me. The dark blobs and pale rings were slowly fading, as if it took effort to maintain. YOU WOULD LISTEN TO OSCAR.

Well, he had me there.

Not-Oscar held up his free hand and, with exaggerated care, reached into his coat. Angus tensed, but the creature only extracted a carefully folded sheet of paper.

WE WROTE A LETTER.

He held it out to Denton. The doctor stared at it. Ingold slid past him and reached out and took it, careful to avoid touching the creature's fingers. He unfolded it, then shook his head. "Too hard to read in this light," he said.

"I got one more question for you, whatever you are," said Angus.

The creature turned its head and waited, slate at the ready.

"What exactly do you *eat*?"

Trust Angus to cut right to the heart of the matter. (It was going to be blood. I was almost sure it was going to be blood.)

Chalk squeaked. WE DO NOT HAVE THE WORD.

"Try," said Angus, in a voice that did not leave a lot of room for linguistic discussion.

I think we all held our breath as Not-Oscar wrote, but I did not expect the answer.

MANY VERY SMALL ANIMALS IN WATER?

That was somehow more bizarre than blood. I had a vague image of the creature crouched over a barrel of sardines. For no good reason, I felt offended. Blood-drinking monsters were something I could understand. I didn't *like* it, but I had *context* for it. An underground monster that ate small fish didn't make any sense and just piled confusion on top of horror.

Angus lowered his gun. "Like fish?" he asked, sounding as confused as I did.

IF THEY ARE VERY SMALL? Not-Oscar started to write something, stopped, then finally held up, WHAT WORD IS SMALLER THAN FISH?

"Christ's blood." I rubbed my forehead. This was the second time that something inhuman and terrible had wanted to have a language lesson, and I can't say that I had particularly good memories of the first time.

Ingold let out a sudden laugh, which echoed shockingly in the tunnel. "Krill," he said. "I'll bet you it means krill or something like that. *You* took the cans of broth, didn't you?"

Not-Oscar nodded vigorously. Ingold turned to the rest of us. "If it's a filter feeder, then it probably can't eat us. We're too big."

"That's a comfort," said Angus dryly. He gestured upward with his gun barrel. "Now what say you that we and our ... err ... *friend* here ... go back up top?"

"Not yet." Denton took a deep breath. "You ... whatever you are ... you can look like other people?"

YES

"Then *stop* looking like Oscar!"

His voice cracked on his cousin's name. I stepped forward, almost involuntarily, and put my hand on his shoulder. He turned away from Not-Oscar, and I thumped his back hard.

Not-Oscar put his slate away and pressed on his face with his gloved hands, pushing it around like clay. Angus made a small noise of disgust. Ingold watched, his mouth open in fascination, as Not-Oscar pushed his chin up and his cheekbones in, then took his hands away. His nose lengthened, like candlewax running, and he reached up, cupped both ears, and pressed them back against his head.

And that was all. He was a different person. Still not Oscar.

"*Incredible . . .*" breathed Ingold, his face alight.

Denton looked up at me and I nodded. He stepped away and pulled his goggles down over his eyes so that we could all pretend he wasn't crying.

"Right," said Angus gruffly. "Now let's get some air and figure out what the hell is going on."

CHAPTER 11

We made our way back to the mine entrance, with Not-Oscar walking obediently ahead of us. At the top, he went straight to the foreman's desk and took out a sheet of paper, then looked at Ingold, possibly for permission. Ingold nodded.

Not-Oscar took a pen in each hand and began to write, and it was immediately obvious why the handwriting on the letters was so peculiar. One hand wrote from right to left, the other from left to right, writing two lines simultaneously. When he finished a line, he simply dropped down and went back the other way, wrists crossing and uncrossing as he worked.

It looked like some kind of parlor trick, or the sort of act that you'd pay a coin to see at the fair. Ingold watched it all with the beatific expression of a small boy who has just been given a puppy. The most amazing thing, to me, was that apparently Not-Oscar could judge exactly how many words fit on a line, which I've never been much good at myself.

A lot of my letters home used to have words crammed up against the edge of the page, to the point where my mother asked if I was trying to write some sort of code.

Denton stood watching Not-Oscar write, the first letter that Not-Oscar had given him seemingly forgotten in his hand. I tapped his shoulder and gestured to the original letter. Denton started, then began to read. I looked over his shoulder, which was rude of me, but given the circumstances, I felt it was justified.

The very first line read: PLEASE DO NOT BE AFRAID.

I stifled an incredulous laugh. Not-Oscar, in his miner's coat and goggles, made an unlikely Old Testament angel, and yet . . .

Shame he didn't appear as a thing made of wings and eyes. We might have gotten off on the right foot if he had.

I glanced over at Denton. There was still hostility lingering in the set of his mouth, but it was being replaced by something else as he scanned the letter. He shook his head at the end, either in bafflement or disbelief, and handed it to me.

> PLEASE DO NOT BE AFRAID. WE HAVE NO HOSTILE INTENTIONS TOWARD YOU. WE WISH ONLY TO BE LEFT ALONE. YOU HAVE STUMBLED ACROSS THE PLACE WHERE WE HAVE SLEPT FOR MANY YEARS. WE WISH ONLY TO CONTINUE TO SLEEP THERE. WE DO HARM TO NO ONE AND HAVE NO ILL INTENT TOWARD YOU OR YOUR PEOPLE AS A WHOLE. WE ARE SORRY FOR ANY ALARM THAT WE HAVE CAUSED.

WE ARE WILLING TO SPEAK WITH YOU AS AN INDIVIDUAL OF YOUR PEOPLE, BUT WE ARE AFRAID OF WHAT WOULD HAPPEN IF OUR PRESENCE BECAME WIDELY KNOWN. THE USE OF MINE EXPLOSIVES HAS ALREADY CAUSED A FRAGMENTATION. WE DO NOT WISH TO BE FRAGMENTED FURTHER. WE WISH TO BE WHOLE AGAIN. OUR KNOWLEDGE OF THE PRESENT WORLD IS LIMITED, HOWEVER. IF WE MUST MOVE OR BE FRAGMENTED, THEN WE WILL MOVE. WE WOULD LIKE TO SPEAK WITH YOU ABOUT THE WORLD NOW. PERHAPS YOU CAN TELL US WHAT IS HAPPENING OUTSIDE THE MINE, AND WHETHER WE MUST PREPARE FOR A MOVE. WE ARE FRAGMENTED NOW BUT WITH ASSISTANCE, WE MAY BE WHOLE.

PLEASE SPEAK WITH US.

"This doesn't seem like a terribly threatening letter," I said. "At least, the bits I understood."

Denton's lips thinned. "Assuming he's telling the truth. This doesn't prove that he didn't kill Oscar. And why look like him?"

"If he was trying to protect others like him, I can understand trying to convince us to go away," I said. "Since you were looking for Oscar, maybe he thought it would be easier to pretend to be Oscar."

Denton met my eyes. "We've been down this road before, haven't we, Easton? A thing that can look like anyone, even the dead."

I swallowed around a suddenly dry throat. In the Usher house, my friend Madeline had been taken over by a being that puppeted her like a marionette long after she was dead. She had referred to it as a child and begged me to protect it. And it had been childlike in its way: as innocent as any newborn serpent, and far more dangerous. It could have made puppets out of the entire human race.

"I don't think it's quite the same," I said.

"We had best hope not," said Denton.

"This is incredible," Ingold said, waving a sheet of paper in our direction. I couldn't tell if he'd heard our conversation or not. "It's world-changing." He laughed, a sound of pure wonder and delight that rang through the cavernous mine entrance. I wondered if such a sound had ever been heard in Hollow Elk before.

Denton looked at Ingold and a trace of fond resignation broke through the hostility. "Well," he said, not quite under his breath. "At least *someone's* happy."

Not-Oscar wrote and Ingold fired questions, most of which I didn't understand. I sat down and put my back against a crate, feeling the strain from crawling and running and horrible revelation. I really wanted a nap, and if you think you can't sleep immediately after something dreadful and life-changing has happened, you probably haven't been a soldier. Angus sat down, his gun in his lap. Denton paced back and forth, aggravated, clearly upset but unwilling to leave. Kent made coffee. All of us, I suspect, were watching Not-Oscar out of the corner of our eyes.

What I pieced together mostly came from listening to Ingold while trying not to doze off.

The creatures were ocean dwellers originally, living on

the surface of the water where it met the air, in a thick gelatinous sheet. ("Some kind of relative of a siphonophore, I think," said Ingold, "but much wider." He looked disappointed when none of the rest of us had any idea what that was.) There it drifted for millennia, changing colors to appear like the sky from below and the sea from above, and so it was able to feed on tiny creatures that rose to the surface.

The creatures were all one creature, but sometimes it broke apart, then came together again. *Becoming whole* was how Not-Oscar wrote it. What one part of a wholeness knew, all of it knew. But if a part broke off and did not come back—because, for example, a whale ate it—it did not make the rest *less* whole.

And there was more than one wholeness.

LIKE YOUR PEOPLE, Not-Oscar wrote, as Ingold tried to get him to clarify. EACH A WHOLENESS.

"Are you a wholeness?" I asked, curiosity pricking through my exhaustion.

NO. He gestured downward, into the mine. WHOLENESS IS DOWN THERE.

Probably they had all started as one, but had literally drifted apart on the tides. A wholeness had learned over vast oceans of time how to use the plasticity of their cells to change into different shapes, and when they met up with another one, the two exchanged pieces and learned all the knowledge held in the other.

I wondered if they ever fought or tried to eat one another. Was that possible? Would they even notice?

Ingold dove in with more questions. Where were these other wholenesses? And how had Not-Oscar's wholeness gotten into a coal mine in West Virginia?

More pages of writing followed. It happened a long time ago. The oceans became colder, and ice crept from the north. The creatures lived on the surface of the water and they preferred warmer temperatures. They could alter themselves a little, adapting to cold and to changes in the saltiness of the sea, and had done so in the past, but actual freezing was fatal to them.

Other wholenesses drifted southward, toward the equator. But this particular wholeness thought that things would become colder yet. It feared that the ice sheets would follow them. So it hatched a different plan. Parts of it had broken off before and explored rivers and undersea caves, then returned to become whole, bringing the knowledge with them. It knew that in caves underground, the temperatures stayed the same, and did not freeze. If it could move itself into one of these caves, it could survive the ice.

"He's talking about the Ice Age!" said Ingold excitedly. "He actually saw it!"

"You mean the one with mammoths and whatnot?" Angus asked, in a tone that indicated he did not approve of mammoths running about loose, regardless of the temperature.

"Exactly! Although it's been proposed that there have been many geological cycles, so it might not have been the most recent Ice Age. These mountains are very, very old." Ingold laughed again. "My god, the things that the wholeness must have seen . . ."

Actually the wholeness hadn't seen very much, as it turned out. It was sensitive to light and dark and could make crude lenses but that was all. Not-Oscar had spent years on his own refining his ability to see and would still be considered nearsighted by human standards. The wholeness might have perceived the blob of a mammoth go by in the distance, but what it *saw* was mostly tiny wiggly things in the water. It had kept to rivers as it oozed its way onto land, leaving the other wholenesses behind. (Ingold peppered Not-Oscar with a great many questions about salinity and salt regulation, but it became clear that Not-Oscar lacked the vocabulary to explain, even assuming that there were words for what it had done. I can't say I followed any of it, and I was glad when he gave up.)

At last the wholeness had entered a cave system, deep enough that it thought it would survive the ice, and there it had gone to sleep, entering a hibernation period where it needed very little food. But it had set a sentry that stayed awake, which would watch over it and fetch food as needed, and which would merge back into the wholeness after a time, bringing knowledge of the world outside the cave, then splitting off again. The sentry would tell the wholeness when it was safe to return to the sea.

And so it had been for a long, long time. Not-Oscar did not know how long. Thousands of years, Ingold said, assuming that it was the last Ice Age. Maybe longer. Because at some point the sentry hadn't come back.

"Wait, you're not this sentry?" I asked, startled.

NO. THE SENTRY IS MISSING.

"What happened to them?" Ingold asked.

WE DON'T KNOW! Not-Oscar drooped in a pantomime of despair. WHY DIDN'T THEY COME BACK?

"Could they have been killed?" I asked. "Eaten by something?"

NOT UNLESS THEY WERE DEVOURED WHOLE.

SOME FRAGMENT WOULD REMAIN AND RETURN. AND THERE ARE NO PREDATORS ON LAND THAT COULD DO SO. He brooded for a moment. A FIRE COULD BURN THEM. OR ANOTHER OF OUR KIND COULD ENGULF THEM, IF THEY WERE SMALLER.

We exchanged uneasy glances. "Are there likely to be others of your kind about?" Angus asked, as if it was of no particular merit.

Not-Oscar started to write something, then paused. After a moment he wrote, slowly: I DO NOT THINK SO. THE OTHER WHOLENESSES THOUGHT WE WERE FOOLISH TO GO ON LAND TO ESCAPE THE ICE. AND THEY WOULD NOT KNOW WHERE TO FIND US. BUT I CANNOT SWEAR THAT IT IS IMPOSSIBLE.

"Did any of you go looking?"

WE DID NOT KNOW. THE WHOLENESS DOES NOT WAKE UNLESS THE SENTRY COMES BACK. THEY DID NOT COME BACK, SO THERE WAS NO REASON TO WAKE.

This struck me as a very foolish system to set up, given everything that could happen to a single individual over the course of what sounded like millennia. Of course, maybe if you were nearly indestructible, you didn't worry about things like that.

I TRIED TO FIND THEM WHEN WE WERE FRAGMENTED, Not-Oscar wrote. I FOUND SIGNS BUT THEY WERE NOT HERE. WHERE DID THEY GO?

Not-Oscar's own fragmentation had occurred when blasting in the mine had triggered a collapse far down in the cave system. Part of the wholeness had sheared off, and though the shock had woken it, it couldn't find its way back.

The smooth, glassy surface that we had encountered was an impermeable secretion meant to keep the wholeness from losing moisture, and Not-Oscar couldn't get through it. The irony of being able to see the object of his desire on the other side of a sheet of glass of its own making was painful, though I don't think he understood irony as such.

"But if it was blasting that did it, then the mine must have been in operation," Denton said. "Which was—what, a hundred years ago?"

It had been more than that. Not-Oscar had seen the second and third shaft sunk. He had watched the miners for decades, first learning that the strange animals communicated through sound, then learning that those sounds mapped onto written words. Apparently one miner had read aloud to his friends during breaks, and that had sparked the initial understanding. After that, Not-Oscar's vocabulary had spread by leaps and bounds, though it never mastered the art of speech. TOO HARD, he wrote. TOO MANY PARTS THAT VIBRATE. (Which made me stop and think about how exactly my lips and tongue worked and the way things moved in my throat, which led to me thinking about how often I swallowed, which is the sort of thing that drives you batty in very short order.)

"How do your people live so long?" Ingold wanted to know, which led to another spate of questions that made very little sense to me. The upshot seemed to be that the wholeness could revert part of itself to ... well, *infancy* probably wasn't the right word. A younger state of sorts. This wiped out that part's memories, but it could then rejoin the wholeness and relearn what it had forgotten.

"So it's effectively immortal," Denton said, sounding

grimmer still. He turned to Not-Oscar with sudden ferocity. "Why are you *telling* us all this?"

Ingold and Not-Oscar stared at him with almost identically blank expressions, as if neither of them understood the question. Not-Oscar wrote, one-handed and somewhat hesitantly, YOU ASKED.

Denton threw his hands in the air and walked away. Ingold looked after him, clearly wondering if he should follow. Before he could move, Kent arose from his seat by the fire and went after his employer. I hoped that he was as efficient in settling nerves as he was at everything else.

Not-Oscar stood very still, holding his slate, and probably it was unwise to project human emotions on what was effectively some kind of a land jellyfish, but he seemed forlorn. I suppose nobody yells at you when you're a jellyfish.

"What do we call you?" I asked the creature. Partly that was to distract it, but it also didn't seem right to keep thinking of him as *Not-Oscar*. "Do you have a name, other than 'wholeness'?"

The creature shook his head. "Wholeness it is," Ingold said.

"What about you, though?" I asked.

WE ARE A WHOLENESS.

"No," I said, "not all of you. *You*. The bit that we're talking to, not the wholeness. The way that I'm Easton and he's Ingold and he's Angus."

Not-Oscar thought about this for quite some time. I wondered if I'd asked a question he couldn't answer, or one he didn't understand. Then finally he picked up the pen and wrote, in his clear, slanting hand, YOU MAY CALL ME FRAGMENT.

CHAPTER 12

In addition to broth, Fragment could eat meat ground into a fine paste, so long as he had plenty of water. This would have made me nervous again, except that apparently he couldn't actually chew, because his teeth were made of the same substance as the rest of him.

TOO SOFT. NO BONES, he wrote. MUST USE STICKS.

Ingold, who had lost all fear in favor of fascination, asked him to demonstrate, and to my shock and horror, Fragment pushed up his sleeve, held out his arm, and it . . . melted. The flesh simply dropped away in gummy strings that dangled below the arm, revealing a stick with bark still attached.

"You've got sticks for *bones*?" Angus said.

Fragment nodded. CAN'T WALK WELL OTHERWISE. As I watched, the long strings hanging from his arm reversed themselves, crawling upward over one another and braiding themselves back into flesh. It was both amazing and dreadful to watch.

It also explained why, when I had seen Fragment flowing along the ground, he had had a human-shaped lump atop him. It had been the bone-sticks and enough flesh to hold them together, while the main body of the creature went slithering along the ground.

It's true what they say, you can get used to anything. It was still deeply, viscerally alien, but my sheer horror was fading the longer that Fragment talked to us.

"So you don't have any teeth either," Ingold was saying, as Denton and Kent returned. Denton still looked tense. (Can't imagine why.)

NO. TRIED ROCKS, BUT THEY JUST PUSH THROUGH JAW.

"He probably *could* drink blood," said Ingold musingly, "though I doubt it would sustain him long. Organ meats processed into a fine slurry would likely work better."

"Is it a coronary you're trying to give me?" Angus demanded.

USED OTHER ROCKS TO GRIND FISH, Fragment offered.

"Fascinating as this is," said Denton testily, "will you excuse us for a moment? I would like to confer with my colleagues in private."

Fragment gave one of his exaggerated nods, and Denton hustled us all outside of the mouth of the mine. I looked over my shoulder and saw the creature standing by the table, hands dangling limply at his sides.

"Can he still hear us, do you think?" asked Denton in an undertone.

Ingold frowned. "I don't think he can," he said. "His hearing is not so good as ours. His ears aren't real. Well, they're real, but they're not real ears. The sounds come in through his entire body."

"I'd think that would make him able to hear better," said Angus.

"Actually, no." Ingold had that enthusiastic light blazing in his eyes again. "Human ears are quite marvelously complicated. They funnel sounds in onto membranes that vibrate against tiny little bones—really, if you took your ear apart, you'd be astonished!"

"No doubt," Angus muttered.

"Fragment doesn't have any of that. His skin can't vibrate the same way because it's busy being skin, and a few other things as well. It's amazing he can hear as well as he does. Or walk, or anything else." Ingold spread his hands. "As far as I can tell, the most specialized cells he has are the chromatophores and the ones that produce the bioluminescent glow. His muscles have to be muscles *and* nerve cells *and* move food around and do all the things that our bodies have specialized cells to do. And that doesn't even get into how they all seem to be some kind of gestalt consciousness, which of course is incredible by itself—"

Denton held up a hand before Ingold could tear off on another tangent. "Did he kill Oscar?"

Ingold blinked a few times. I could practically hear the squeal of brakes being applied to his train of thought. "There's no way to know," he said finally. "He was certainly in the mine. He clearly saw Oscar up close, although that could have been at any time. His eyes actually do work, interestingly enough; he says that he studied a dead possum's eyes and figured out how they worked, although he's using pond water in place of aqueous humor—"

This time I was the one who broke in. "Is he the one who's been killing people over at the camp?"

Denton turned his head toward me sharply. I spread my hands. "It was the bit about organ meat turned to slurry. The corpse we saw had its organs pulled out like someone shucking an oyster."

"I'd be very surprised if he was," Ingold said. "He doesn't have real bones."

"You don't use your *bones* to kill people," Angus said dryly.

"You do, though." Ingold's eyes started to light up again and Angus threw me a look of exasperated amusement. "Most of your muscles have to have your bones to anchor them and to push against. Imagine . . . oh . . . trying to punch someone with your tongue. That's what it's like for Fragment."

There was a pause while we gave this particularly vivid mental image the credit it deserved. I opened my mouth to mention a young lady of my acquaintance in Paris, but caught a glimpse of Denton's expression and closed it again.

"Fragment's using a makeshift wooden skeleton so that he can walk," Ingold said, "but he's significantly weaker and slower than a human. The only way that I can see him overpowering someone is if there was a lot more of him somewhere."

Angus spoke for all us when he said, "Huh?"

Ingold glanced around at us. "Surely that occurred to you . . . ?"

"I think it's fairly safe to say that you're ahead of us again," said Denton wearily.

"Well, there's no reason that he has to be the size of a human, is there?" asked Ingold. "We know that the wholeness itself is huge. How big was the chunk broken off? There could be a room filled with Fragment somewhere that he rejoins occasionally."

I can't swear to it, but I suspect that Denton and Angus and I were all forcibly reminded of the tarn and the fungal intelligence within it. It had sent out bits of itself to possess the bodies of hares and . . . other things . . . which then returned to the dark water to rejoin the larger body.

"We know he can use tools," Ingold said blithely, "so if there was a lot more of him, he wouldn't really *need* bones. He'd just need to engulf someone until they suffocated, then scrape the guts out with a sharp knife."

There was a second pause while we contemplated this image. I did not like it. Judging by their expressions, neither did anyone else.

"How do we find out if there's more of him?" Denton asked.

"You could ask him." Ingold shrugged. "He's been remarkably forthcoming so far."

"*If* he's telling the truth," Denton said. "Hell, he's not even a he, is he? He's an it."

Everyone looked at me for some reason. (Fine, I know the reason. I'm just saying that Angus speaks Gallacian as well as I do. They could look at him instead.) I rolled my eyes. "Don't ask me. Gallacian doesn't have anything for . . . I don't know, intelligent land-jellyfish." (Granted, if any language would, it would be ours. Still.) "He's choosing to appear as male, so *he's* as good as anything."

Ingold rubbed the back of his neck. "Anyway, I don't get

the impression he's lying about anything. I don't think he understands lying very well."

"He was *pretending* to be *Oscar*." Denton's voice sounded as if it had been chipped out of flint.

"Yes, but that wasn't a *lie,* exactly." Ingold frowned. "It was mimicry. Imitating something isn't the same. His— err—species imitates things all the time, I think. If a shark was coming toward them, they'd pretend to be another shark so that it wouldn't try to eat them. It's more defensive. Even the telegram he sent was basically mimicking Oscar so that we wouldn't come back."

Denton grimaced. Ingold hurried on. "I'm inclined to think he's exactly what he says he is. If nothing else, it's too *weird* to lie about."

The doctor folded his arms. "Have you learned enough to know how to kill him?"

Ingold blinked. "What?"

"*If* he killed Oscar and *if* he's responsible for the killings over in the camp, we're not just leaving him here to keep doing it. So how do we kill him?"

"But the loss to science—"

"Science be damned!" snarled Denton. "I'm not leaving a murderous—whatever that is—loose!"

"Why is everyone's first response to a stranger to kill them?" Ingold shot back, his hands clenching into fists.

Now seemed like a good time to put my foot in it. If nothing else, I could give both of them someone else to be mad at. I held up both hands and stepped between them, in the pose colloquially known as "the first one to get punched."

"Stand down, both of you," I said. "Nobody's killing anyone right this minute, alright? We don't know that Fragment's done anything to anybody. And even if we wanted to, we can't get through that shell over the wholeness, unless somebody's been smuggling dynamite in their trousers."

The joke fell flat but I kept talking anyway. "Ingold, you yourself admitted Fragment *could* be dangerous. I'd like to know how we protect ourselves if he is. I don't think that's terribly unreasonable, eh?"

Ingold grimaced and looked over my shoulder at Angus. Angus said, "It's a fair question, lad. Knowing how doesn't mean we've got to do it."

Oh sure, when I say it I get glared at, but if Angus says it, suddenly it's sweet reason.

"Shooting him won't do much," said Ingold reluctantly, not looking at Denton. "It'd damage the tissues in the immediate area of the wound, that's all. And there'd be even less point in stabbing him. He said fire would work."

"*If* you believe him."

"Fire works on nearly everything," I pointed out.

Denton grunted. Ingold folded his arms. "I really don't think he means us any harm."

"Then what *does* he want?"

Ingold looked up with an awkward smile. "Actually, I think he needs our help."

"He wants us to open up a hole to more of them?" I asked.

"He can't do it himself," Ingold said. "The way his muscles work, and as hard as the stuff is, it would take him centuries to drill through by hand. And dynamite would hurt the wholeness." Ingold put a thoughtful finger to his lips.

"Of course, he was using a plain steel bit. It's very possible that with one of the new diamond bits, we could—"

"No!" Denton snapped. "*Absolutely* not. Isn't one enough?"

"He *isn't* one, though," Ingold said, "he's part of a group and he's been cut off from it. It's like bringing a bee back to the hive."

"Yes, by opening the door to a swarm of bees!"

He and Ingold stared at each other, neither backing down. I shuffled a half step back, not wanting to get in the middle of the competing glares. Angus gave me an I-see-what-you're-doing look, cleared his throat, and said, "We don't have to decide right now. Let's have some dinner, shall we?"

I looked around, startled, and realized that dusk was already lurking in the corners of the cavern. "That's a good idea!" I said, with false heartiness. "I'm famished."

We ate in silence. Kent presented Fragment with a cup of chicken broth, which Fragment accepted, writing THANK YOU on his slate. I imagined all sorts of horrible ways he might eat the stuff, but he simply drank it out of the cup, although he never seemed to swallow.

As soon as he was finished, Denton put his dishes down and stalked out of the mine. I was nearly done, so I said, "My turn," and went after him.

He hadn't gone far, just out of sight of the entrance. He glanced over at me and I waited to see if he was going to tell me to go away. I don't think he knew either. Hope dies hard at the best of times, and Denton's hope had died harder than most. Eventually he sighed, took a slug from a small silver flask, and told me to pull up a rock.

We sat in silence for a while, while the insects buzzed

and rattled in the trees. Denton took out a cigarette and patted himself for a light. I pulled out my lighter and flicked my wrist to snap it open and light the flame in one motion. (If you do it right, it looks very suave. I used to practice it for hours as a teenager, in hopes of impressing girls.) (Look, girls were more easily impressed in those days. Shut up.)

"I hate this," Denton said. "I hate this so much."

I stretched out a hand and he pressed the flask into it. It was bourbon, which I don't much care for, but we weren't drinking for aesthetic appreciation. I downed a slug and passed it back.

"Do you remember what it was like, coming home after the war?" Denton asked unexpectedly.

"Of course."

He took another sip from the flask. "Home is where you're supposed to be safe. But if something like that could happen, then how could any of us be safe anywhere?"

I grunted. It hadn't been quite like that for me, but I understood it. Meanwhile, the whippoorwill had started up and was caroling monotonously somewhere out in the darkness.

"But I got over that, you know? It took some time, but I stopped expecting someone to burst through the door and demand that I operate *right now*. I could come home and close the door and just . . . be there."

I grunted again. I don't have many social skills, but I can tell when someone is spilling their guts and I should keep my mouth shut and let it happen.

"And then, after Usher's lake . . ." He gestured vaguely eastward with the flask, presumably toward the site of our shared horror. "I kept thinking that if creatures like that existed, no one could ever be safe anywhere again. Anyone could turn out to be one of them."

"Yeah."

"It was like I couldn't go home. I kept waiting for the door to open and something horrible to come through." His laugh was soft and humorless. "It wasn't until Ingold convinced me that something like the tarn wouldn't happen twice—that we'd killed it and it was really *over*—that I was able to feel safe again." He pressed the metal of the flask against his forehead, perhaps to cool it. "And now it's happening again. Except that my dearest friend is on the side of the monster this time. I feel like I'm going mad."

"You're not," I said. "This is all . . ." I tried to find a word and failed miserably. Denton nodded, though. Maybe we'd come to a place where there were no words in English or Gallacian to describe what was happening to us.

"Yeah," he said. "Yeah." He stared at nothing for a little while.

"Am I ever going to be able to go home again?"

I knew he wasn't talking about Boston. I didn't have an answer. I realized that I hadn't heard the whippoorwill for some time.

I was trying to think of something that I could say that would give Denton a small slice of strength, enough to get through the next little bit of hell, when we heard the horses screaming.

The sound of a horse in panic will bring a former cavalry officer to their feet if they're dead asleep, dead drunk, or just plain dead. Being none of those things, I was tearing across the hillside to where we'd picketed the horses before the echoes of the first scream had died away.

I was the first one on the scene, but since I'd neglected to bring a light, all I saw was a dim, confused jumble of plunging horses. Angus was second, and he'd had the wit to grab a lantern. The light bounced as he ran, briefly illuminating glimpses of long legs and eyes rolling frantic white—and a great dark shape clinging to the back of the nearest, something huge, with long clawed arms sunk into the screaming horse's sides.

Angus and I fired at the same moment. One of us hit. (Probably Angus. My shot went high, I'm sure, since the last thing I wanted to do was hit the horse.) The shape jerked, clung for a moment longer, then retreated off the far side. I say *retreated* because it wasn't a fall. I could almost see it *decide* that this wasn't worth it and choose to leave.

I gave chase for a dozen steps, then stopped, confounded by the darkness and the shadows of the trees.

"It got away," I said unnecessarily, returning. "But it's injured. We should see blood in the morning, maybe we can track it."

Angus grunted. He was already trying to soothe the creature's victim, who was not inclined to be soothed. Kent joined us a moment later, and between the three of us, we managed to quiet the horses, although they were still skittish and jumped at every movement. (I felt much the same way.)

"Was it a bear?" Denton wanted to know.

"It didn't look like the bears we have in Gallacia, but yours are small and black, aren't they? So maybe?" I shrugged helplessly. I hadn't seen any details at all, not even the gleam of eyes. "It was a damned strange thing, anyway."

The mare—my mare, as it turned out—was not badly hurt. She had two long slashes raked across her ribs on either side, but it looked as if the creature had only just secured a grip before we ran it off. Denton and Angus did what they could, and Kent made plans to take her back to the livery stable in the morning so that she could get better care than we could offer out here.

In all the excitement, we'd almost forgotten Fragment. Or at least, I had. It wasn't until I was preparing for bed that I heard Ingold and Denton arguing in low voices.

"Fragment was with me the whole time."

"*That* bit of him was. You said yourself there might be more."

"I asked him. He said he could barely feed as much of himself as there was. He's almost completely hollow inside, did you know that?"

"And you believed what he said?"

"Denton, he'd have no *reason* to—"

"That we know of."

I pulled the blanket over my head to drown them out.

In the morning, even though we scoured the hillside, there was no trace of blood to be found.

CHAPTER 13

Denton was dead set on Ingold not being alone with Fragment and since not even I believe that I'm more competent than Angus, he stayed with them while Kent took the mare back and I accompanied Denton to check on his patient with the mangled arm.

It was a lovely crisp fall day. The leaves, already brilliant, were glowing in shades to eclipse even the most extravagant dye. Elijah was glad to see us, and Denton went inside the shed while I sat on the step and petted the hound again.

In daylight, it was clear that she was female. I had just found the spot to get her hind leg going when she suddenly leapt to her feet and gave a thin thread of a whine, then vanished under the steps.

"Something wrong, girl?" I leaned over to look at her. She came out of her hiding spot, barked almost soundlessly at me, then retreated. (In Dog, this means, *Yes, something is wrong, and you should be hiding.* If she'd meant

Something is wrong and you need to fix it, the bark would have been much louder.)

A moment later, my ears caught the crunch of feet on gravel, and I watched Roger and his dog approach. Christ's blood, but that beast was enormous. For a moment, I wondered—but no, dogs bite out the throat and the belly, they wouldn't leap onto a horse's back. And even as gigantic as Thunder was, he wasn't the size of the thing I'd seen the night before.

Roger waved to me and I lifted a hand. Thunder didn't look in my direction, which was just as well.

It wasn't until they were gone and the brown hound had emerged, ears flattened, that I wondered if the reason I found Thunder so unsettling was that his ears didn't move at all.

Denton's patient was recovering better than he expected, so he was in a good mood as we returned, but it faded as soon as we reached the mine. He saw Fragment and Ingold together and his lip curled up as if scenting something rancid.

"He hasn't done anything hostile," I said.

"I don't trust him. He's not human. What's to say he won't just turn on us without thinking twice? Not out of malice but because . . . I don't know . . . it's the season where they all murder each other."

"I suspect Ingold would have learned if a season like that existed by now."

Denton hunched his shoulders deeper inside his coat. The thought crossed my mind that some of Denton's hostility was not directed at Fragment so much as at Ingold and Fragment *together*.

Which was a thought that tied back to some other things I'd half noticed, and made me wonder... *No. None of my business.*

Nevertheless, an hour or two later, when Fragment wrote that he wished to visit the wholeness, I volunteered to go with him before Ingold could.

"It's fine," I said. "I don't mind."

I couldn't help but notice that Denton didn't object to Fragment and I being alone together. Possibly he thought that I could defend myself more effectively. Or possibly... no, *still* none of my business.

ARE YOU UPSET WITH ME, ALEX EASTON? Fragment wrote after we'd threaded our way into the tunnels on the third level.

"Eh? No." Which was true. Overall, Fragment seemed so harmless that it was hard to stay frightened. My gut kept insisting that he wasn't a threat. Denton would probably say that my various body parts had no experience with something like Fragment, and he wouldn't be wrong, but it was still hard to overrule the feeling. It had kept me alive too many times.

I APOLOGIZE. I STILL DO NOT READ HUMANS WELL.

"Oh." I rubbed the back of my neck. "No, it's not you. It's all the weight overhead. It bothers me."

He stopped. SHOULD WE GO BACK?

"No, no. I'm used to it." I kept walking. "Sooner we get there, the sooner we get back up."

WHY DID YOU COME IF YOU DO NOT LIKE THE STONE?

"To prove a mountain can't tell me what to do."

I DO NOT UNDERSTAND.

"Neither do I," I said, sighing. "But I'm here anyway."

I did let Fragment go down that undulating tunnel of a crawl space without me. Denton could yell at me if he didn't come back. But it's not as if Fragment was our prisoner. How do you keep a prisoner that can ditch his bones and turn into goo?

He returned an hour later, re-forming himself out of the narrow opening. I caught a glimpse of clear wet slime sliding into the coat and filling it out, and looked away. My skin crawled, but my gut said, *It's only Fragment.* I wondered which one of them I should be listening to.

"Ready?" I asked.

YES. THANK YOU. Fragment paused, then added, I CANNOT TOUCH THE WHOLENESS, BUT IT COMFORTS ME TO KNOW THAT IT IS STILL THERE.

"I feel the same way about Catholicism," I said, and explaining that kept me talking until we reached the main shaft.

Voices came from above as we made our way upward. It took me a moment to place one as Roger. "... an' I thought on what you said, Doc, and Mister Oscar, he never would have given up on me, and here I was givin' up on him and myself, too."

"Stay human," I murmured to Fragment, who nodded.

"I'm glad you're doing better," Denton said.

Fragment stepped out of the shaft ahead of me. I was looking up, seeing his shape silhouetted against the light, when something happened.

I heard a roar, the sound of running feet, and a shout, and came out of the shaft at exactly the wrong moment. Or exactly the right one, depending on how you look at it, I suppose.

Fragment half turned, his body starting to melt away, and all I could think was *Christ's blood, don't let Roger see!* I jumped in front of him, and then something huge and heavy barreled into me, knocking me backward. It felt like I'd stepped in the way of a galloping horse.

I don't think it was expecting resistance, and I certainly wasn't expecting to be hit, so neither of us were in control of the next bit, where we fell back into the shaft, rolled over several times, and then I somehow wound up on top, straddling . . . a dog?

It was Roger's dog, Thunder. Teeth gleamed white in the dark, snaking toward my face. I shoved myself back, still not certain if I was injured from the initial blow or not. I didn't want to hurt a dog, but Thunder clearly didn't feel the same way about me. Those teeth snapped shut an inch from my face.

Christ's blood, I thought, *it's rabies.* I jammed my arm into the dog's throat, trying to pin him to the ground, but the beast heaved and nearly threw me off entirely. How was it so big? I would have sworn Thunder was a large dog, but the animal under me seemed as big as a pony.

"No!" someone was saying. "Bad dog! Bad dog!" I recognized my own voice after a moment, for all the good it was doing. I managed to get my arm across Thunder's neck and threw my whole weight against it. The next snap of the teeth was farther away from my face, although not nearly far enough.

"Fragment, get out of the way!" Angus shouted, and I thought, *Oh thank God, Angus can shoot it before I get rabies, too,* then remembered that I was fighting a black dog in a dark mine shaft and any relief was probably premature.

The dog heaved again, and then something happened in the vicinity of his chest. Something very bad. I was still wearing my headlamp, so I saw, with horribly clarity, how his sternum pushed upward and then split in half. Long black strings unbraided themselves from bone and the bones themselves pushed forward. I had a sickening glimpse of Thunder's ribs, and then they were no longer ribs but jagged teeth in a vertical maw, knitted together by slick black flesh that writhed away like gums.

I would like to tell you that, in that moment, I knew that it was no dog at all but the missing Sentry. But clearly I *didn't* know, because I could still hear myself screaming, "No! Bad dog!" and the horror at what I was seeing was all mixed up with a horror that *I* had somehow caused this, had broken the poor beast's ribs myself and sentenced him to a lingering agony.

This lasted right up to the point where the new mouth flexed upward and bit into my gut.

The thick oilskin coat saved me. I felt the jagged bone ends clutch at me, seeking purchase, felt them slide along the fabric, and then a gun went off so close to me that powder burned my skin and I fell backward off the thing that clearly wasn't a dog at all. (Fine. You had probably figured that out already. My only defense is a fundamental belief that dogs are inherently good and Thunder must therefore be good and if he hadn't liked me, it was probably a failure on my part.)

I have a great belief in the stopping power of bullets. Mostly I believe that they don't stop nearly enough. Certainly this one didn't. The bullet went through not-Thunder's head and blew out the back, trailing black strings behind it. But by the time I had scrambled to my feet, the strings were already reknitting themselves, and though the head looked as if one side had been crushed, the rest of the creature didn't even seem to notice.

At that moment, I should have run away. I was aware of that even at the time. But I was furious—deeply and unexpectedly furious—because how *dare* this monster impersonate a *dog*?

I think I screamed something to that effect, but probably it was in Gallacian. Nevertheless, Sentry faced me, even as it reared up on impossibly long legs. Christ's blood, it really was huge. Thunder hadn't been that big before, I would swear it. It shook itself and the mouth in its chest flexed again, and in a voice that was half-bark, half-gurgle, it cried, "*I—will—not—be—whole!*"

Angus—of course it was Angus—fired again, and the creature staggered but didn't fall. It turned toward him, snapping both sets of teeth, and gathered itself to spring.

"Out of the way!" shouted Ingold, and with the courage I'd always suspected he possessed, he flung himself between Angus and Sentry, far too close, so close that the upper teeth actually closed over his arm, but he didn't falter. His free hand came up holding an oil lamp, and he smashed it down over the creature's back.

Burning oil ran over it and it fell back against the wall and slid downward. Ingold tore his arm free and slapped at the splashes of oil on his clothes. The burning Sentry was between me and them, so I had no idea how badly injured he might be.

What I *did* see, with horrible clarity, was how Sentry dealt with burning. Its skin rose up like dozens of fleshy fingers, more strings pulling away from bone, and then it simply sloughed half its body away. The burning half fell to the ground and the creature dragged what was left of itself away from the fire, sacrificing its own flesh to smother the flames.

A beam of light carved an erratic zigzag over the wall. I half turned and saw that it was a headlamp bouncing on the ground, rolling down the shaft. Fragment's headlamp, followed by . . . Fragment's pants? I'd thought the creature had fled, but apparently he'd just been undressing. Then Fragment himself pushed by me, still changing as he went.

His flesh pulled away. The sticks that made up his bones clattered to the floor. By the time he reached Sentry, he was only vaguely human-shaped. He lifted his arms and a thick membrane hung down from them like wings.

He fell over what remained of Sentry, arms outstretched, and I watched the membrane flow over the other like a second skin.

Sentry struggled wildly against Fragment's smothering embrace. I saw the thrashing as Fragment enclosed him in a translucent sac, and could see the outlines of bones punching against the membrane. I took a step forward, wanting to help, not knowing how. It soon became obvious that my help wasn't required. Sentry had been huge, but he had lost half of himself to the flame, and now Fragment was twice as large as he was.

I staggered past them, up the shaft to where Angus and Ingold were watching. Angus had his gun out, but Ingold pushed it down with his good hand. "I don't think you should break Fragment's . . . err . . . seal right now."

"What's he doing?" I asked. And then, "Christ's blood! Your arm!"

"I'll need stitches," he admitted. He had his arm pressed against his side. "But it could be worse. And in answer to your question, I think he's . . . ah . . . engulfing him. Eating him. Or merging with him, if you like."

"But that thing's a murderer! And pretended to be a dog!"

"Yes," said Ingold. "But Fragment outnumbers him right now. Presumably that will dilute some of the . . . well . . . *murderousness.*"

Red light flashed inside the sac, irregularly at first, then slowing to a dull red pulse as Sentry's struggles died down. We stayed well back. From the top of the shaft, I heard Roger saying, "But my dog went down there—" and Kent's voice answering, too low to make out. Good. Keep him away from all this and we'll make up a story somehow.

Then more footsteps, and Denton was there, holding a lantern and a box. No, one of the box-shaped oilcans. He pushed past us, lifting it up, and it took me a moment to realize that he intended to douse both the creatures with it.

"No!" I grabbed for him, missed my footing on the slope, and skidded practically into Fragment before I stopped myself. "Denton, stop! Fragment's *got* him, it's under control."

"That's both of them there?" Denton asked. And when

I nodded, "Good. Then we can deal with this once and for all."

And he pulled the cap off the oilcan.

I am not always the quickest person on the uptake. I said, "Err, what?"

"He means to kill them both," Ingold said. "Denton, no. Think of what you're doing!"

"I am thinking. I'm thinking we have them both here, at once, and we can end all of this right now."

I darted a glance over my shoulder. Fragment and what was left of Sentry were still lying in a heap of undistinguished flesh. They couldn't get away, and if Ingold or Angus grabbed for Denton, he'd spill the oil or drop the lantern and set them on fire anyway.

Which meant the only person who could stop him was me.

Was I really going to risk being burned alive to save an alien being more closely related to a jellyfish than a human? Apparently I was. I spread my arms and said, "Denton, don't do this. This isn't right."

"I never thought *you'd* balk at doing what was necessary," Denton said coldly. "You of all people."

"*Necessary*, yes," I said. "Fragment saved my life just now. You want me to pay that back with murder?"

"My cousin is *dead*."

"And now we know what did it," Ingold broke in, "and Fragment's dealing with it. Oscar's at peace. We can be at peace, too."

"*Peace?*" Denton sounded incredulous. "When it's down there, able to look like any of us, just like that thing in the lake—"

"It's *nothing* like the thing in the lake," I shot back. "You've met Fragment. He's had years to practice and he still couldn't pretend to be one of us for more than five minutes. He won't last ten minutes outside the mine."

Denton didn't look convinced. I tried another tactic. "Denton, I don't know what oath they make doctors swear over here, but in Gallacia, ours says, 'First, do no harm.'"

The oil gurgled as his hand trembled on the oilcan. Angus met my eyes over his shoulder and looked a question at me. I shook my head. I couldn't see any way to rush Denton that didn't end with somebody being burned alive. Probably me.

"We could end all this now," said Denton finally, his voice cracking. "We could stop it and just go home."

It was the cry of every soldier I'd ever served with. *Just let this stop happening and let us go home!*

I'd like to say that I said something eloquent, that I made the argument that changed Denton's mind, but it wasn't me. It was Ingold who put his hand on Denton's arm and said, very gently, "That's all Fragment wants. To go home to his people. Let us help him, and then we'll go home to ours."

"You don't want that," Denton said miserably. "You think this awful alien thing is *wonderful*."

"I would give up every wonderful thing to go home with you," said Ingold.

Denton let out a sob and turned and Ingold's arms went around him, which confirmed a few things I'd been wondering about, and Angus, sensibly, took away the oilcan.

CHAPTER 14

Fragment reassembled an hour or so later, which was just about enough time to finish explaining everything to Roger. I would have preferred to skip that bit, but he'd gotten past Kent and seen enough not to be put off easily. Also, there was the matter of Thunder.

"You said you found him near the mine?" Ingold asked.

"Yeah. Ate like a horse, but the best dog. Watched over me drunk or sober. And you're saying this thing *replaced* him?"

Ingold and I exchanged glances. "It's possible that it always *was* him," Ingold said gently.

"But he was a dog!"

"This creature could look like a dog."

"But why'd it look like *my* dog?"

We went around on this three or four times, until Fragment finally appeared and Ingold gratefully seized on the interruption. "Did you learn anything?" he asked.

NO. SENTRY DID NOT WISH TO JOIN WITH ME.

"What does that mean, in practical terms?"

I DO NOT KNOW. IT HAS NEVER HAPPENED BEFORE. BUT I WOULD NOT FORCE A JOINING. He wiped the slate clean and wrote, COULD HE HAVE GONE MAD FROM LONELINESS?

"Uh . . . I'm no expert on your people, Fragment. I don't know."

"Happens to humans," I offered.

BUT HE DID NOT HAVE TO BE ALONE! Fragment underlined the word *BE* twice. I could see a faint red radiance coming from the skin that wasn't covered by clothes or goggles.

Ingold got the hunted look of a man trying to explain psychology to an alien jellyfish creature. (It's rare, but you know it when you see it.) "It's complicated, Fragment. Sometimes when people hurt for a long time, they start to think that hurting is part of who they are. And then anything that helps the hurt, even healing, feels like it's trying to strip part of them away."

This gave both Fragment and I something to think about. Roger, however, was not given to such introspection. "But why'd he take my dog?"

Fragment wrote, PERHAPS HE WAS LESS LONELY BEING YOUR DOG?

I bit my lip. Ingold winced. Roger stared at the slate, blinked twice, then burst into tears.

"It's all right," I told Fragment wearily, after Kent and Angus had taken Roger away to recover himself. "You didn't know."

BUT I DID NOT MEAN TO DISTRESS HIM!

"I know you didn't." I patted his arm, unthinking, and felt the flesh give a little too much, which made me realize that I'd treated him as I would an upset human. It's true what they say, I suppose. You can get used to anything.

I suppose if settling into pleasant debauchery doesn't work as a career, I can hire myself out as an alien ambassador.

Ingold stepped into the written recriminations and said, "Fragment, I've been meaning to ask why you glow red sometimes. That was what let us find you in the first place."

Fragment turned his goggles in Ingold's direction. IT IS LIKE HUMANS TALKING, he wrote. IF A HUMAN IS ALONE, IT TALKS TO PRETEND ANOTHER HUMAN IS TALKING.

I started to protest that that wasn't why humans talk to themselves, then realized I couldn't possibly explain all the nuance, then further realized that I didn't understand all the nuance myself, and shut my mouth.

WHOLENESS GLOWS. Fragment tapped the chalk against the slate. I wondered if that was an actual nervous tic or if he was imitating something he'd seen humans do. I DO NOT ALWAYS REALIZE I AM GLOWING.

"An unconscious behavior," murmured Ingold. "Fascinating. But I'm curious about the mechanism. Can you glow deliberately?"

Red light began to leak from Fragment's skin in answer.

"Amazing. And is this a specialized kind of cell, or . . . ?" Ingold and Fragment rapidly descended into jargon, all about "bioluminescence" and Saint Elmo's fire. (In Gallacia, we call it "the candles of St. David.") I gave up and went out to check on the horses, to find Denton already there.

The doctor flushed when he saw me and looked away. "Easton . . . Alex . . . I . . . ah . . ."

I held up a hand. "You didn't do it. That's all that matters."

He stopped, cigarette halfway to his mouth. "Err . . . but I did do it. Many times."

We stared at each other in baffled silence. "I'm talking about dumping oil on me and Fragment."

"*Oh.* I meant . . . um. John and I." He was turning red behind his beard.

"Oh, *that.*" Christ's blood, did he think I cared? Americans were so bizarre. "Denton, I do not know about anyone else's military, but if half the Gallacian troops weren't tossing each other off occasionally, I'd worry they weren't getting enough to eat."

Denton's explosive snort unfortunately coincided with him taking a puff of the cigarette and he choked. I pounded him on the back until he could breathe again. The horses eyed us with grave suspicion.

"I mean, *that,* yes," the doctor said. "But I didn't know he felt that way. I thought it was just that . . . well, I was there, and convenient. We didn't talk about it."

"And now you know. So that's all right, then." And now we were talking about feelings. I would almost rather he had poured the burning oil on me.

Denton grunted. I slapped him on the back again and fled.

"It's odd," said Ingold at dinner that night.

"What's odd?" Angus asked. (I almost asked what *wasn't,* but restrained myself.)

Ingold shrugged. "Just . . . why was Sentry taking all that meat? That much food would last Fragment for a month."

TWO MONTHS. AND IT WOULD TAKE DAYS TO INGEST.

"I thought you said they couldn't eat meat," Denton said accusingly.

"No, I said they couldn't *digest*. Something like our stomach acid would eat right through them. But Sentry was actually very clever—he used gizzard stones!" He looked around at us triumphantly. I attempted to look suitably impressed, but clearly failed, because Ingold sighed and said, "Like a bird. He made a crop, filled it with rocks, and let them roll around and grind the meat up. Then when the pieces were small enough, they'd pass into a water-filled stomach and become something he could ingest. And of course he was using an actual skeleton so he could chew it to begin with. In fact, he'd made some modifications to the basic canine skeleton. I imagine that when he first began killing the people at the shantytown, he was taking bones as well as organs."

I put my food down and pushed it away.

I HAD NOT EVEN CONSIDERED SUCH A THING. Fragment frowned. SENTRY WAS MUCH SMARTER THAN I AM. AND HE COULD EVEN TALK A LITTLE. I DO NOT KNOW HOW.

"I wonder if he had a syrinx, like a bird," Ingold mused.

"You're not out there stealing other creature's bones," said Angus, before Ingold could launch into a treatise on comparative avian anatomy. "That's the important thing."

IT IS?

"Rules of life," Angus said. "Be true to your friends, don't cheat at cards, don't piss on the less fortunate, and don't steal other people's skeletons."

"You just added that last bit now," I said.

"Obviously should've been there all along." He leaned back. "Now then, gents, since we can't use dynamite, how do we propose to get Fragment here back together with his people?"

I'll spare you the details of the next few days, since most of it was spent tracking down a diamond core bit. (Apparently most of them are attached to steam-powered machines. Who knew?) It was a good thing we were in coal country, because Kent eventually found one. If we'd been in Gallacia, he'd still be looking. Ingold and Fragment stayed thick as thieves, but in the evening Ingold would stop and go sit outside with Denton. I assume they were working out the details of their old-turned-new relationship. I also assumed that it was none of my goddamn business.

The diamond bit cut nicely into the shell around the wholeness. It still wasn't *easy*, mind you. Everyone took a turn turning the drill handle and cursing. But it made an inch and then another inch and then another and then we all sat around with aching arms and tried to ignore the white faces in the floor, mimicking our expressions. (Denton didn't take part in this. No one blamed him. He was trying very hard, and at least he knew his limits.)

"Why do they do that?" asked Ingold, gesturing at the brilliant floor. We had brought blankets down to sit on, partly because the floor was hard but mostly because it was extremely unsettling to sit on a floor that was imitating you.

The blankets looked very small and shabby in that pearl and limestone chamber of so much glory, and I clung to mine with deep relief.

IT IS PROTECTION. IF A SHARK COMES, THE WHOLENESS LOOKS LIKE A LARGER SHARK SO THAT IT WILL NOT BE FOOD. EVEN DREAMING, THE WHOLENESS PROTECTS ITSELF. Fragment waited until we had read the slate, then wiped it clean and began writing again. WITH MOST BEINGS, IT IS ENOUGH TO LOOK LIKE THE HEAD OR EVEN JUST THE EYES.

"Oh, of course!" Ingold slapped the blanket. "Like the moths with wings that look like big eyes to scare predators away. The wholeness tries to look like a bigger human to frighten us off."

Several pearlescent versions of him celebrated this, open-mouthed with delight. I looked away.

"We're running low on water," Angus said, turning his canteen to hear the slosh.

"I'll go get some," I volunteered. I didn't like the crawl, but I'd gotten used to it, and now it was only skin-crawling, not vomit-inducingly awful.

We'd all gotten a little lackadaisical about going around the mine in pairs by this point, so no one stopped me. I made my way out of the tunnels, back to the main shaft, and began whistling an old Gallacian tune about the milk-maid and the virtuous wolverine.

I had just gotten to the bit where he offers to scratch the itch she cannot scratch herself when I heard a grinding noise and looked up.

A wall was falling slowly on top of me.

It was a wall of flesh, not stone. It extruded itself out

of the mouth of the second-level shaft, grabbing at the ground and pulling itself forward with things that were not quite tentacles but definitely not feet. It had dozens of eyes and hundreds of mouths that opened and closed and re-formed elsewhere on its body. Bones stuck out and were turned into hooks to keep dragging itself forward, yard after yard of anonymous meat pouring out of the tunnel, seemingly with no end in sight.

Ah, I thought, very calmly, *so that's what Sentry was doing with all the extra meat.*

Meat seemed like the best word. It was the color of old fat and it fell apart and re-formed in dangling, gelatinous strands.

It saw me a moment after I saw it. Most of me wanted to stand around and shriek, but the part of me that survived far too many battles spun me around and sent me running deeper into the mine.

Not down! I thought miserably, even as I ran. But I couldn't possibly get past it. It filled the central shaft of the mine to capacity. My only hope was to lose it in the tunnels on the third level.

I scrambled back into the open tunnel mouth, and realized almost immediately that I would not be losing the rest of Sentry anywhere. It was faster than I was, and already practically at my heels. A smear of flesh whipped out and struck me across the back, sending me stumbling. I suspect that the only reason I survived was because it took longer to turn corners than I did.

The white beam of my headlamp skidded over a familiar three-way junction.

Right was a dead end. Left took me back toward the

others. But they were down in the cave with the wholeness, and even if I survived long enough to reach the spiral crawl space, Sentry would pour down it and devour first me, then the others.

The middle tunnel was low and tight, and the word *firedamp* and something less than a plan slid through my brain together.

I dove into the middle tunnel.

I made it perhaps ten yards in before something whipped around my ankles and I fell. I hit the ground and thrashed, kicking at the coil of flesh trying to encircle my shins. I managed to get one foot loose and rolled over, gasping in . . .

Not air.

Everything slowed down. I crawled backward on my elbows . . . at least, I thought I was crawling backward on my elbows, and watched as a ball of pale flesh lurched through the tunnel and landed on my foot. The underside of it was black with dust. A fragment of bone emerged from the ball and stabbed down into my calf. From a long distance away, I screamed.

In your pocket. Get your hand in your pocket. That's all you need to do.

I told my hand to get into my pocket, but I had no idea if it was happening. Controlling a whole arm seemed an impossible feat. Ingold had said that Fragment had to control each muscle individually, and I had never really appreciated how hard that must be. I would have to tell him the next time I saw him.

You're not going to see him again. You're going to die here. But get your hand in your pocket first.

The shapeless lump of flesh stabbed another bone

fragment into my leg, just above the knee, and I realized that it was climbing me like a mountaineer climbing a peak, using the bones like pitons to brace itself against. I was probably still screaming, but it all seemed very far away.

I felt cold metal under my fingers. That seemed very odd.

Grip it tight. The voice in my head sounded a little like Angus. I wished that Angus was here. No, wait, I didn't wish that. If Angus was here, the monster would be eating him, too.

The squeeze began to fill as the bulk of Sentry's horrible second body reached the tunnel and began pushing itself inside. Translucent shapes like sea anemones flowered around the opening, then grew darker and more opaque as more of Sentry rushed to fill them.

I hitched my body backward, despite the excruciating pain in my leg. (Surely it was excruciating? I didn't like to think I'd be screaming so much otherwise.)

The headlamp beam no longer showed stone overhead, only writhing flesh and protruding bone. It loomed over me like a great wave and hung there for an impossible moment. I clutched the metal thing in my hand and thought *rectangle* and *cold* and I didn't mind dying, not really, but did death have to look so revolting?

The wave came crashing down.

Everything went dark. Something clammy pushed against my lips and nostrils. It really was a good thing that I was only partially tethered to reality anymore. Otherwise I would find this very disturbing.

Now put out your hand, said the voice that wasn't Angus.

I tried, but there was something in the way. The voice

wasn't impressed. *Push, then. Don't let go of what you're holding.*

So I pushed. Muscle parted in front of my fingers. My right hand went through the monster as if it were made of dough. Occasionally it would hit something thicker, stalks of tendon or bone.

Keep pushing! It was starting to sound like my first drill sergeant now. I wished it would make up its mind.

Something was going up my nose. Maybe when it got to my brain, it could tell the voice to pick an identity and commit.

My fingers hit air, then stone.

Now, said the voice, and this time it was my father. *Alex, do it now.*

Do what?

But the advantage that I had over Sentry was that my muscles only had to be muscles, and they remembered things, and what they remembered was a great many hours spent practicing as a teenager, so that when you have a metal lighter in your hand, you push your thumb like *this* and flip your wrist *just so*.

Click.

There was a sound so loud that I couldn't hear it and I felt myself lifted an inch or two in the air.

My last thought before I lost consciousness was that if there were any girls around, they'd be really, really impressed.

CHAPTER 15

"... down any second," someone said, very quietly.

"I don't care," Denton snapped. He was only a little louder, but he sounded angry. "The rest of you get out and let me work, then."

I couldn't make out what was said in reply. Could I open my eyes? I experimented. They would only go up about halfway, but I could just make out the blurry shape of Denton crouched over my legs.

Legs? Yes, I had those, didn't I? Could I move them?

I tried. My mistake became obvious when pain struck me like a bright light and everything went gray and floaty for a bit.

"... be ridiculous ..."

"I am telling you, if we move them, there's a chance that

bone will hit an artery and either they bleed out or I slap on a tourniquet and they probably lose the leg."

I wondered who they were talking about. Not me, obviously. I was dead.

Though I admit, I hadn't expected being dead to hurt so much. Clearly the priests had been lying to me.

"What do you mean?"

I cracked my eyes open again and saw Denton. He was looking very intently at something. No, someone. *Oh, hello, Fragment. You're here too.*

I hoped this didn't mean that they were both dead. That would be sad.

Fragment was writing something on his slate. I squinted but couldn't read it.

"It just has to stay in place until we get Easton up top."

Wait, they were talking about me?

Somebody else said something, but it sounded like a gnat's buzz in my ears. Denton didn't look away from Fragment. "You're *sure*? If it's already plugging the artery and you accidentally dislodge it . . ."

Fragment held up the slate. I really wished I could see what was on it. This was starting to sound important.

Buzz buzz buzz went the gnat. Christ's blood, couldn't people learn to speak up?

Denton's expression was something I had never seen before, hope and horror in equal mixture.

"Do it," he said. "Start with the lower one."

Nothing seemed to happen for a little. Then my calf began to itch like the devil. The itch was interestingly distinct from the pain, and I didn't like it at all.

I tried to reach down to scratch and Denton snarled,

"Hold them down, you bastards—no, not like that! Do you want to puncture a lung?!"

Something pressed hard on my shoulder. I managed to turn my head a little and even through the glare of the headlamp, I'd recognize Angus anywhere.

"Hold on, youngster," he said. At least I think that's what he said. I could barely hear it, so I had to read his lips while not being able to quite focus my eyes. It might have been *Hold on, chicken coop*—the words are similar in Gallacian—but that seemed like an odd thing to call me.

My leg still itched.

"Jesus, Mary, and Joseph," Denton said. "Yes. Do the other one."

The itching suddenly got about a thousand times worse. I tried to scratch again and then there were more hands holding me down and Denton barking orders and everything was terrible and if I could just scratch, I could deal with it, but no one had warned me that being dead would *itch*.

I tried to tell Angus about the itching, but he just patted my shoulder and didn't seem to hear.

"Now," said Denton. "As smooth as you can."

The hands holding me shifted and now they were lifting me up, up toward the ceiling of the mine, and then through the ceiling and into the stone and the darkness.

"You," Angus said, "are proof that God looks out for fools and drunkards."

"I resent that," I said. Actually I nearly yelled it, then had to consciously lower my voice. My hearing had mostly come back, but not all the way. Denton wasn't sure if I'd ever get the rest back. "I am *not* a drunkard."

Angus snorted explosively and helped me to my feet. I picked up my cane and began limping toward the back of the cavern, where Fragment was waiting.

It was Fragment who saved me when the firedamp ignited. I would have suffocated long before they were able to drag me out, but the creature had made himself into a kind of tube and burrowed through the burning remains of Sentry until he could reach me and plaster himself over my nose and mouth. He fed air through until they were able to clear the fallen rubble and pull me free.

Angus wasn't wrong. I'd had God's own luck. Sentry's body had shielded me from the worst of the firedamp explosion and the falling rock. My injuries from fighting a monster and blowing up part of the mine amounted to a cracked rib, two admittedly nasty gouges in my left leg, and some burns on the side of my right hand. And the possibly permanent hearing loss, which would at least pair nicely with my tinnitus.

Of all of it, the burns were the worst. Burns hurt like nothing else. Denton had done his best and was changing the dressings every day, but my little finger was already hardening into a crooked claw.

Oh well. At least it's not my trigger finger, and it's not like my handwriting could get much worse.

Sentry was truly dead. What hadn't died in the blast was doused with lamp oil and set ablaze. (Served him right for pretending to be a dog.) Angus, Fragment, and Ingold had swept the second floor of the mine while I was recovering. They'd found another, smaller pocket of Sentry, and this time Fragment had overwhelmed it and taken its memories by force. I had the impression that doing so was upsetting, but he had no body language to read. Maybe I only hoped he found it upsetting.

TRYING TO BECOME A NEW WHOLENESS was Fragment's analysis of Sentry. Perhaps even becoming large enough to destroy the wholeness slumbering peacefully below. Something between a city and a god, made up only of himself.

There were bones jumbled inside Sentry's various bodies, some of them being used, most of them broken past all recognition. A ring had turned up in the second pocket, which Denton identified as Oscar's.

Denton and Fragment had made their own peace. Angus said that he thought it was in the hours when they frantically hauled away rubble, trying to reach me, while Fragment had been funneling air to keep me alive. "He didn't know what to do about the bleeding," Angus had said, rubbing the stubble on his jaw. "Pretty soon Denton was shouting orders at him like a raw recruit, and it stopped mattering that he was basically just a tube and a pair of hands writing on a slate. Then we actually got to you, but the ceiling was maybe about to come down. Denton really didn't want to move you, but Fragment did something. Must have worked because we got you up top without killing you, and then Denton started yelling that we were all useless except Fragment, and for god's sake, just get out of his light and let him work." Angus had nodded then, clearly satisfied with the results.

It's rare that you can mend relationships with an explosion, but I'll take it.

(Ingold had to explain to me what Fragment had actually done, which was apparently to insert an incredibly thin layer of himself into the wounds with the bones stuck in them, then slowly thicken the layer until the bone popped out. Then he plugged the holes with his own flesh until Denton could operate. The thought made me a little queasy, but not nearly as queasy as seeing just how close one of those holes was to the big artery in my leg. No wonder Denton had been yelling.)

I reached the edge of the shaft, where Fragment stood waiting, with Ingold and—perhaps surprisingly—Roger beside him.

IT IS GOOD TO SEE THAT YOU ARE RECOVERING, ALEX EASTON.

"It's good to *be* recovering." I glanced down into the darkness. "I suppose this is goodbye, then?"

"We broke through the shell this morning," Ingold confirmed.

PART OF ME WENT BACK AT ONCE, Fragment wrote. BUT I WANTED TO LEAVE ENOUGH TO SAY GOODBYE. He paused, tapping the chalk absently against the slate. AND TO THANK YOU.

"You, thank me?" I snorted. "You saved my life. Twice."

AND YOU SAVED THIS FRAGMENT'S LIFE. TWICE.

"Well, then that probably makes us even."

Fragment's eyes were hidden behind the goggles, and perhaps even then, they would not have conveyed any information. The eyes are the window to the soul, they say. Did Fragment have a soul? I thought he probably did, and that was as much as I could say for any person I knew.

THERE IS NO DEBT IN A WHOLENESS, he wrote finally. I WOULD OFFER WHOLENESS TO YOU, IF SUCH WERE POSSIBLE. BUT I DO NOT THINK YOU WOULD WISH SUCH A GIFT.

"I'm afraid not," I said, repressing my shudder at the thought.

Though I couldn't help but glance at Ingold and wonder if he would pass up such an opportunity.

I took a step back and nodded to Roger. "You'll be okay here? Errr... both of you?"

Roger had elected to stay and guard the mine, "in memory of Mister Oscar." (So he said, anyway. I suspected that he was actually staying in memory of Thunder. Despite our best explanations, I don't think he truly believed that his dog had never really existed in the first place.) Regardless, Denton had offered to pay him a wage to watch over Hollow Elk and see that it remained undisturbed. After we left, he would board up the entryway more firmly, with the help of...

Well, of the new Sentries. Which would contain Fragment within themselves, no doubt, as well as the rest of the wholeness. Fragment had been very clear that there must always be two in the future, to watch each other as well as the mine.

I HOPE WE WILL BE VERY WELL, ALEX EASTON.

"I'll send books," Ingold promised. "You'll never be bored."

Roger muttered something under his breath.

If I could have walked down into the mine without a cane, I still don't know if I would have gone to see Fragment rejoin the wholeness. It felt a little like death to me, poor singular creature that I am. But the choice had been taken out of my hands, so Angus and I watched the trio's lights dance as they made their way down the shaft.

We stood for a moment in silence and listened to the sounds of the mine breathing out, a slow, peaceful sound like a dreamer deeply asleep; then I began the long, slow shuffle back to the entryway.

Denton was waiting for me there, shadowed by the faithful Kent. "Have they gone down?" he asked.

I lowered myself onto a camp stool. Kent handed me a cup of coffee. "They have," I said.

"Well. That's good then." Denton too had made his peace with what slept beneath the mine.

"And will you be able to go home, you think?" I asked. We had tickets for the train tomorrow morning, but as I knew well, there are ways that you can and can't go home again.

Denton nodded slowly. "I still don't like thinking that there's things like that Sentry out there," he said. "But Fragment's potentially a better surgeon than I'll ever be." He shook his head. "I'll get over the one, but probably not the other. Every time I see a patient that could be saved if I could do what he did . . ." He shook his head again, a wry twist to his lips. "Pretty sure that'll haunt me to the grave."

"You could try to convince some of him to come with you," I said. "Maybe he'd like to be a doctor."

"And explain it to the nurses? No, thank you. Three can keep a secret if two of them are dead, and we're at least three over. Hell, I'm not that sure about Roger. I'm just hoping that if he talks, everyone will assume he's drunk again."

"You can always come back and check on things," I offered.

"I expect to be doing so regularly. Fortunately, Elijah

over at the camp has offered to contact me if it looks like Roger is...ah...taking his duties less than seriously. And of course the new Sentries will know how to send telegrams as well." He leaned back. "I admit, I didn't expect to be tasked with taking care of something like this for the rest of my life, but I suppose someone had to do it."

"Who better?" asked Ingold, appearing out of the darkness. He dropped down next to the fire and accepted coffee from Kent. Denton put an arm around him, and he leaned into it with no trace of self-consciousness. "I certainly wouldn't suggest the American government handle it."

"Their record with things that aren't...ah...part of their wholeness isn't good," Denton agreed.

"Christ's blood," I muttered, trying to picture it and failing utterly. "They'd probably try to send the poor bastards to Guam."

"Did everything go...eh...?" Angus made a grasping gesture with one hand that was probably meant to convey a creature rejoining its long-lost group mind. This was not a concept that lent itself to hand gestures. Nevertheless, Ingold nodded.

"I think so. At least there were no explosions."

Everyone looked at me. I rolled my eyes. You blow up *one* mine shaft...

"You're welcome to stay with us in Boston for as long as you like," Denton said. "Do some sightseeing. See more of America. Whatever you like."

"I mean this in the nicest possible way," I said, "but I think I have seen enough of America to last me for a while."

"The parts outside of mine shafts are generally much nicer."

"Mm. So you say." I looked over at Angus. "What do you think?"

He shrugged. "Seems a shame to come all this way and not at least look around."

I sighed deeply. "Fine. We can stay in America for a week or two. But I am not going into any more mines."

"Sure," said Denton.

"I don't even want to go into a cellar."

"That's fine."

"And if anything weird happens, I am getting back on the boat."

Ingold grinned at me. "Come now, Alex, what are the odds of something else this strange happening in the next week?"

But that, as they say, is another story.

Acknowledgments

My favorite story by H. P. Lovecraft is *At the Mountains of Madness* because it's so rare that you can use an art history degree in a horror novel. There is more wrong with Lovecraft than I could begin to enumerate in a month of Sundays, but I liked the art history and the albino penguins, and I also liked the shoggoths.

Fragment and the wholeness came about because I started thinking about how I'd make a shoggoth from spare parts lying around Earth. Obviously, it would start with a sea creature, and I figured it would be something rather like a siphonophore, which can do all kinds of neat tricks, crossed with a jellyfish, which can do even more neat tricks. Much gratitude to Rebecca R. Helm, oceanographer, who consulted and said that I was getting into cephalopod territory in places, but she'd allow it.

Even more gratitude goes to my old friend David Rodland, who took me seriously when I asked about geology and cave systems in West Virginia. I took a lot of liberties

ACKNOWLEDGMENTS

that may make him wince, but it was extremely valuable to have that framework to work from.

Much of my information about coal mining and various damps came originally from a slim volume called *Coal Mine Disasters of North Carolina* by John Hairr, who probably never expected his work to inform a horror novel, but which was extremely useful. I would not have known what questions to ask without it as a starting point.

And, of course, thanks as always to the team at Tor Nightfire, who do such good work, and my editor, Lindsey Hall, who makes the books much better than they would be otherwise.

For my readers—okay, yes, the dog sorta dies, but it wasn't really a dog, so hopefully that makes it okay? I agonized, but at the end of the day, like Easton, I came down on "How dare a monster pretend to be a dog? That is not okay! Dogs are sacred!"

Last but far from least, my husband, Kevin, is the reason that books get written and I don't simply die under a pile of dirty laundry. Also he, too, spent hours learning to flick a Zippo lighter to impress girls. Never let it be said that art doesn't imitate life.

T. Kingfisher
Edgewood, New Mexico
2025

About the Author

JR Blackwell

T. KINGFISHER writes fantasy, horror, and occasional oddities, including *Nettle & Bone, Thornhedge, A Sorceress Comes to Call, What Moves the Dead,* and *A House With Good Bones.* Under a pen name, she also writes bestselling children's books. She lives in New Mexico with her husband and a yard full of completely ordinary rocks.

"Any new T. KINGFISHER book is reason to take a personal day."
—NPR

"Like nothing else on shelves." —*Paste*